HUNTER'S RULES

DI HUNTER WILSON CRIME THRILLERS: BOOK 6

VAL PENNY

SPELLBOUND BOOKS

First Published by Darkstroke.
RePublished 2024 by SpellBound Books

PRAISE FOR VAL PENNY

Val Penny is a star of the tartan noir fiction genre. In this story of drugs, injury and lies, the author delivers yet another gripping book in her DI Hunter Wilson Crime Thrillers series.

Erin Kelly bestselling author of He Said/She Said

This dark mystery pulls together a full cast of characters, some lovable and some perfectably unlovable, and sweeps them away on a journey with plenty of unexpected turns. Dry wit and humor in the face of misfortunate bring the pages to life until the satisfying conclusion.

Elizabeth Lyvers, bestselling author of The Honest Lies

Another winner, courtesy of Hunter Wilson and Val Penny.

You're hooked within the first few words, whether it's with Hunter's love life, or latest case.

The story hits you from the very beginning, and keeps you hooked all the way through to the end, with plenty of twists and turns, not to mention breath-taking moments, as you would expect from such a great storyteller.

Simon Hall of Cambridge University, bestselling author of The TV Detective series.

This is a gruesome story told within the beautiful city of Edinburgh. You walk the streets with a strong cast of police and villains. Two murders a few months apart: an injured woman in a fine hotel and the manipulation of weakness. A great holiday read for all crime fiction fans!

Michael Jecks bestselling author of The Knights Templar Mysteries

A gripping read. When Val Penny asked me to do an advanced read for Hunter's Rule, I was a little dubious at first because it wasn't my normal genre. However, I'm glad I agreed. The story grips you from the start. Penny keeps the reader guessing and turning over the page. An unputdownable book.

Patricia M. Osborne, bestselling author of the House of Grace Saga

Hunter's Rules kept me on the edge of my seat! It was a satisfying mystery, but hearing some of the bad guy's plans, seeing all the relationships between characters, and the non-stop action kept me drawn in.

Jessica Thompson, bestselling author of A Caterer's Guide to Love and Murder

To John, Lesley, Scott and Stewart
with love

CHAPTER ONE

Detective inspector Hunter Wilson rose from the table and led his girlfriend, Doctor Meera Sharma, from the exclusive Pompadour Restaurant towards the elevators in Edinburgh's Waldorf Astoria Hotel.

"That was a delicious meal, thank you, Hunter."

"You're more than welcome, dear. It was good, wasn't it? My steak was so tender, I could have cut it with a spoon. Oh Meera, I do love you and I'm so glad your father consented to our marriage."

"So am I. I know I don't need his consent, but life will be much easier because he approves. It was kind of Parvati to take the time to teach you some Hindi."

"I've arranged to continue my lessons with her, so that I can communicate with all the members of your family."

"Hindi is a demanding language to learn for a non-native speaker," she said.

"Maybe, but there are almost six million people who speak it, I can't be stupider than all of them."

"Time will tell, darling." She grinned. "Thank you for learning some, anyway. I admit I was worried at first. I really thought you and Parvati were having an affair when I first heard about you sneaking about together."

"I'm not an idiot, Meera. Parvati is wonderful, but compared to you, she is like a star to the sun. Anyway, I make it a rule not to shit on my own doorstep," Hunter said.

"Oh yes, Hunter's rules. I forgot." She fingered her sparkling engagement ring and smiled. "So much to celebrate. Can we go public?"

"Not yet, pet. Let's wait until it's announced in the newspapers and all official."

"It's going to be difficult. I'm so proud I think I might burst."

"Well, I have just one more surprise for you."

"Another one? Oh Hunter," she said.

"I've booked the honeymoon suite here for us tonight, and if everything has gone according to plan there should be a bottle of champagne chilling there for us. Shall we go upstairs and check?"

Hunter and Meera continued walking towards the elevators, and he pressed the button indicating they would be going up. They stood close together, gazing into each other's eyes, but it was not long until the furthest lift arrived. They shifted slightly towards those doors and make room for anybody getting out.

Nobody got out.

A young woman lay motionless on the floor and the inside of the car was drenched with blood.

"Oh God, not another one," Hunter said. He stared at the

raw flesh in the sockets where the girl's eyes should have been. What kind of monster would choose to murder someone this way? He turned away from the horrific sight of the young woman's butchered face. He gagged. Then swallowed the bile. He daren't contaminate the crime scene with his own vomit.

Meera knelt beside the victim and felt her wrist. "Hunter, this one is still alive. Call an ambulance. Do it now!"

Hunter immediately went into professional mode. He stepped a few yards away from the scene and called the ambulance. The soles of his shoes were covered in blood. Then he phoned Fettes Police Station. Desk sergeant Charlie Middleton answered.

"Police Scotland, how can I help?"

"Charlie, the eye thief has struck again."

"Fuck."

"Succinctly put. This one has survived. The ambulance is on its way. Can you get a team together right away to start questioning witnesses here and we'll need the CSIs pronto."

"Great, just one question."

"Come on, Charlie. Time is of the essence, man."

"Yes, Hunter, but where is here?"

Bloody hell, that was close. I hadn't expected her to be found so soon. That's bad luck. I thought she'd have time to bleed out and die like the others. What are the odds that a damn policeman would be dining at the same time as us. We must be paying them far too much. I'll have to work for a week to put that money back into my savings.

I have to say, her eyes are even more beautiful than the others.

They are the same peculiar violet colour that Elizabeth Taylor's were. Not that I ever met Elizabeth Taylor, I don't mix in those circles in America, but I've seen pictures.

I'm pleased that I brought my jar filled with solution with me. I won't have time even to go into my room, let alone fondle myself in front of her eyes before I pass them on. Wow what a coming that would have been. I'll have to imagine those eyes now.

Fuck, I'm so angry. Who would have believed my luck that the first man on the scene would be police? This is too bad.

It's a good thing I sussed the place out before we met. I'll go down the stairs and out through the public bar. In fact. I'll stop for a drink there, then I'll get a bus, not a taxi. Fast enough but hard to trace. I need to get them to him quickly, but I must remember to keep my head down.

The ambulance arrived faster than they could have hoped, but by that time the injured woman was moaning. Meera knelt beside her ignoring the blood stains on her dress. Ignoring the compromise of the crime scene. The woman took priority.

"Why is it dark in here? Why are my eyes sore? Where's Frederick?"

"Don't worry about anything just now. You've had a shock. An ambulance is here to take you to the hospital. I'm a doctor. I'll come with you," Meera said softly. She patted the woman's hair.

"Meera, the paramedics are here," Hunter said.

She moved away to give the paramedics space. They gave the woman painkillers, and she was soon unconscious again.

"Christ!" the female paramedic said. "Is that the same attacker?" She looked at Hunter for an answer.

"I can't say anything. You know that, but it looks like it. Same MO. If it is he may have made a mistake this time. She's alive."

"We'll try to keep her that way. Are you coming, Meera?"

"Yes, I'll come. I don't want to leave her."

"I'll stay here and keep people away from this lift. I'm glad it's in the corner. I'll let you know when the CSIs and uniforms get here, Meera." Hunter kissed her discreetly on the cheek and nodded towards the patient. "Look after her."

Meera followed the paramedics towards the ambulance. She noticed they had covered the woman's face, to protect her from prying eyes and mobile phones. They made it to the Royal Infirmary of Edinburgh in record time. Blue lights and sirens cleared the way. Meera was relieved to see that Ailsa Myerscough was one of the doctors on duty.

"Bed four," Ailsa said to the paramedics. Handover in two minutes, I just want a word with Dr Sharma. I understand she found the victim."

"What the hell, Meera? Tim seemed to think Hunter was taking you for a romantic meal."

"And he did. We were waiting for the lift to take us up to the honeymoon suite of the Waldorf Astoria when we found this young woman."

"What's happened?"

"Her eyes have been gouged out. The whole eyeball."

"I've read a couple of women have died from similar injuries recently. Is it the same perpetrator do you think?"

"Too early to tell, but if it's not, we have more than one sick assailant in the city. I think the only thing that saved this girl is that Hunter and I found her so soon after the attack."

"Anything else you can tell me?"

"She hasn't been told the level of her injury yet but before she was given the painkillers, she asked why it was dark, why her eyes hurt, and she also asked for 'Frederick'."

"I take it Frederick was nowhere to be seen. Okay, thanks Meera. I'll go and do the handover with the paramedics now. Do you want to stay?"

CHAPTER TWO

Hunter was pleased to see DC Neil Larkin arrive. He was always a safe pair of hands. "Over here, Neil." He waved. "I'm glad you're here. The smell of this lift is giving me the grue."

"Nice to see you too, boss. CSIs here yet?"

"No, but they're on their way. I'll go to get the manager to put this lift out of commission, now. I think because it's the corner one we can get away with that. Then the CSI team can finish their work in peace."

"I'm surprised it's not already officially out of use," Neil said.

"Thanks for that. I was here waiting for you. No, sir, I'm sorry this lift is out of use." Hunter showed the guest his identification. "This keeps happening. People always coming over. We'll need to get this area taped off. Is Charlie on his way?"

"Here Hunter," Sergeant Charlie Middleton said. "I pulled rank and got our car parked in the hotel carpark. I'll get the area isolated."

"Good thinking. Charlie. Hello, Scott." Hunter said as he noticed DC Scott Clark following Charlie. He was gazing around the foyer of the hotel smiling at the shimmering lights and fittings.

"Scott," Hunter repeated. "Earth to Scott."

"Evening, sir. This is posh, isn't it?"

"Are you here to work or admire the décor?" Hunter asked.

"Sorry, boss. The sarge says you need us to take witness statements."

"Exactly so and here comes the cavalry," Hunter said. He smiled at Chloe Ferguson who was known as Fergie. She led her team of CSIs towards him. He looked at her grim expression.

"We'll need to get this done pronto so the hotel can have their lift back. Of course, it must be thoroughly sanitised before it's back in use," she said. "Anyway, Sam's on her way. We'll let her get her initial photos taken before we start. It looks like someone's danced on the floor. Look at those bloody footprints in the car and all over here." She pointed to the marks on the shiny polished floor.

"Sorry, Fergie. Hands up, that was me and Meera. We checked if the woman was still alive and when she was, Meera did what she could for her while I called you and the ambulance."

"For fucks sake, Hunter. You know better."

"I did as little damage as I could, but the victim was in a lift."

"I know, I know. It's just lucky the professionals are here now. Oh, and there's Sam. Let's give her space."

Hunter watched the quiet photographer get her equipment ready and set to work.

"Neil, if you stay here and keep everybody away from the elevator. No mobile phone photos or films either. See anybody taking any you just confiscate their phone as containing evidence. That'll stop the rest fast enough. Charlie, you and Scott take statements from the staff on duty in the bar and restaurant tonight. The guests too. See if you can get any descriptions of the woman and whoever she was with."

"As we don't know what either of them look like or names or anything, can you give us a clue, boss?" Scott asked.

"The woman mentioned the name Frederick. She has dark hair and was dressed in a fancy red velvet dress. A cocktail dress, I think they call it," Hunter said. "I suppose there wouldn't be too many red velvet dresses."

"What are you doing here anyway?" Charlie asked.

"I was treating Meera to dinner, if it's any of your business."

"Well, it is. If you were having dinner at the same time as the victim, you could be witnesses. Did you see her?"

"No, not that I remember. Bugger, I'll have a think and write you a statement. Right now, I'll go and find the manager, to bring him fully into the loop before the press get wind of this. Then can I leave you in charge, Charlie? I'm over the limit and need to get home for a sleep. Looks like I'll be in tomorrow, whether I'm meant to be or not."

Charlie went to find the maître de table who oversaw the restaurant. He did remember the woman in the red dress. The man had booked the table. His name was shown on the booking as Frederick Carver. He had left a mobile telephone number. Charlie made a note of both, but experience told him not to expect either to prove fruitful.

Scott took details from all the staff and initial statements.

One waiter said that the couple looked as if they were on a first date. The man took the lead in all things and insisted the lady be given a guest menu which had no prices on it. He ordered the drinks and another of the waiters recalled that the man paid in cash. He remembered that because it was unusual in the Pompadour. Most guests charged their meals to their room or put it on their card.

A waitress remembered other details that Scott thought might be useful. The man had dark hair and a full, bushy beard. She remembered that the woman seemed drunk when she left the table to use the ladies' room. She had seemed alright until then. Certainly, when she got up she walked there and back, a bit wobbly, but she went alone. However, when the couple left the table shortly afterwards, the man had virtually carried her out. She certainly couldn't walk.

Scott was surprised by this and wondered what could have happened to explain this sudden change. Maybe the wine had gone to the woman's head.

CHAPTER
THREE

"It was good to see your pop," Frankie said to Jamie. "But they were a bit late letting the cons in, weren't they? What did your pop say, again?"

"Some toerag was found with a sim card in his mouth. Rookie error. Anyway, it right did him good to see us and hear about how your wedding plans are going."

"Aye, I said we're no' having it til he's out the big house. So that's why we've no told the twins yet. They're too wee to understand. They'll be bonnie as our flower girls, won't they?"

"And with me being the best man I get to make a speech about what a nob you are." Jamie laughed. "It makes me nervous that Donna's asked Linda to be her bridesmaid. They're bickering about the colour of her dress and the like." He became serious. "I just hope it doesn't give Linda any ideas about her and me."

"My guess is that ship has long sailed," Frankie said.

"Probably." Jamie shrugged. "I don't suppose there's any chance you want to let your Mam know, Frankie? Auntie Edna would be happy to hear you're settled and doing so well."

"You suppose right. I've told my bro, of course. Harry doesn't know where he'll be or if he'll be able to get leave to come even. It depends where he is and what he's doing."

"Problem of being in the army," Jamie said. "And the fact you haven't actually set a date."

"What did your pop say to you when he sent me off to get the coffees? He made sure I had to queue up in two lines to get his chocolate as well. And I had to walk to the vending machines on the far side of the prison visiting room. He was up to something. I know him."

"I suppose you do. But he does like a bit of chocolate." Jamie changed the subject. "It always smells the same, in that visiting room; disinfectant and sweat."

"A pongy combination at the best of times, and that wasn't one of them. Why did you and your pop have to mention my fucking mother? May she rot and burn," Frankie said. "I was in a right bad mood thinking about her as I stood waiting for the machines to give me the drinks and Uncle Ian's chocolate."

"He was only trying to be nice. And I tried to smooth things over."

"He wasn't and you didn't. But you'll never guess who I saw."

"Who?"

"Arjun Mansoor. How could I have worked for that evil man for so long and noticed nothing?"

"Dunno. Maybe you're just thick."

"Shut up, Jamie. Mansoor had a right shiner. His left eye was all black. I was buggered when your pop told me why he got it. But nothing happens in HMP Edinburgh without him knowing."

. . .

Jamie nodded and thought back to the private chat he had had with his pop.

"Look son," Pop said, "while Frankie's away, let me tell you something. I think that house is getting too crowded with you two lads having your girlfriends there and what with Frankie's twins and everything. There'll be no room for me when I get out and it won't be that long now. I'm keeping my nose clean this time."

"That makes a change, Pop."

"None of your cheek, lad," Ian said. "At least I've no' been caught." He grinned at his son. "Have you still got that money we stashed when we sold the hearse?"

"Of course. But that's not got a lot to do with keeping your nose clean."

"Shut it, we need to sort this before Frankie gets back. Is it in Thomson's Top Cars?"

"Aye, where else did you think it would be? Of course, me and Frankie took our cut like you said, rest is in the safe in a Tesco bag."

"That's good. But what I wanted to tell you is, I've heard that Mr and Mrs Morrison who live in the other half of your semi are moving soon."

"How could you possibly know that from in the clink?"

"Mansoor knows them. He was talking. I'm sure they'll move a bit faster if you make their lives difficult."

Jamie grinned and shook his head. "You're impossible, Pop. But I can do that easy enough."

"And use that chunk of change for the deposit. Feed to the brief, little by little, that way there'll be no money laundering questions."

"You sure Pop? It's a hundred grand remember. That's enough cash for a right good deposit, I'd guess. We could buy it outright if you'd let us use the money from the business"

"Well just do that. It can be a company asset. Hush here comes Frankie. Don't tell him about the new house, it'll be a nice surprise."

"What did he say again?" Jamie asked Frankie as they got into the car to drive home.

"I said that Mansoor's got a black eye and how'd he get it? Your pop said he was talking out of turn about the twins."

"Your twins? What does he know about Kylie-Ann and Dannii-Ann?"

"He knows the Morrisons who live next door to us, and they'd been telling him about them. He was winding Uncle Ian up, so he gave him a thumping in the showers."

"The bastard. Won't he complain?"

"Not if he knows what's good for him. You know what your pop's like. It was right nice of him to stick up for the twins," Frankie said.

"He always will."

"I heard they're planning to move house soon. Could we maybe look at getting their place for you and Linda? It'd be good to have you next door, but our house is getting right crowded."

He watched as Jamie burst out laughing. "What's so bloody funny?"

"Come on, Frankie. Let's stop for a pint and I'll tell you."

CHAPTER FOUR

Tim Myerscough felt his phone vibrate in his pocket. He looked at the screen. Why was Lucky, the formally named Lord Lachlan Buchanan, phoning him? One way to find out.

"Lucky, what can I do for you?"

"Timmy, boy, thank God you haven't changed your number. And thanks for picking up, I know I'm not your favourite person, but I didn't know who else to call."

"Does that make me first choice or last choice? On second thoughts don't answer that. What do you want? And by the way, you're more likely to get it if you don't call me 'Timmy boy'."

"Sure of course, Tim. I'm just nervous."

"Nervous is not a word I normally associate with you, Lucky. Selfish, greedy, manipulative, unpleasant, any of those but not nervous. Anyway, aren't you still in rehab?"

"Yes, but that's just it. I'm due to get out in a couple of days if I can get a reputable person to sign me out and take me home. Back to the estate and..."

"I'm the only reputable person you know?"

"Not exactly..."

"Why can't your ever loving cousin Felix help you? I admit, he's not terribly reputable, but that's not generally known in public circles. I thought he was living out at the estate too. It would be much more convenient for him to do the needful."

"That's the thing. You see he's gone AWOL. Switched his phone off and everything."

"Never a good sign with Felix," Tim said.

"You're right there. Probably means he's off to Ibiza or Marbella looking for fresh meat or DJing or both. Anyway, I can't get in touch with him."

Tim thought for a moment. He disliked Lachlan, but they went back a long way. He couldn't see him stuck. Then he had a lightbulb moment.

"What about the lovely Lady Sophie Dalmore? You and she used to be an item. Sophie will help, surely."

"I haven't heard from Sophie since my conviction. She doesn't take my calls and no letters."

"She's probably a bit busy to be writing letters to her drug addled ex-boyfriend, I suppose."

"That's harsh, Tim."

"Harsh maybe, true, definitely."

"Also, did you know her dad died?"

"Yes, a shock being so sudden. I'm going to the funeral to pay my respects, tomorrow. She'll be involved with arranging that. It'll be a bit of a change seeing Geoffrey as the new Lord Dalmore," Tim said.

"Send her my love and kindest regards, won't you?"

"I think I'll pass on being your messenger in her hour of grief if it's all the same to you. However, if there's nobody else in your little black book who's willing to help you out, I'll pick you up and take you home. But I'm not accepting any responsibility for you after you get out of my car."

"Agreed. Thanks Tim. You're a true friend."

"I wouldn't say that. Look Lucky, I've got to go, I've got another call holding and this one's from somebody I actually like."

There really are some right bloody toffs in the police now. I mean look at Tim Myerscough. With a pedigree and wealth like his and a first-class degree, he should be right at the top of the pole now. But no, the bloody goody two shoes won't use his wire or even take the fast-track graduate thing. He wants to show everybody that he can do it all on his own.

Good looking bastard probably can. I know the funds he inherited from his mother are enough to allow him to buy and sell most of us. But that won't save his girlfriend. Apparently, she has the most vibrant green eyes. Nice.

"Hi Gillian, what's up, pet?" Tim asked.

"Hi honey, I've just got an email from the university in Moscow."

"You've been waiting for that. What's the offer?"

"I've been offered a year's teaching contract."

"A year?"

"Well, an academic year. Nine months. I'd be teaching my favourite topic, eastern European languages, Russian, Ukrainian, Uzbek, Georgian, Slovakian, Slovenian and Czech and the nuances and changes that have developed since the countries separated. It's a great opportunity, Tim."

"Starting when?"

"Summer term. I'd start in April. It's a lovely time of year in Moscow."

"If you're doing summer term to summer term it'll be almost the year, unless you plan to come home for a while."

"No, I wouldn't. I'd start work on the courses running the following academic year. I'd want to do my own research too."

"That's what I thought. Look, you can't pass up on this this opportunity. Can we speak about it tonight at home? Maybe you can give some thought to what you want to do for your birthday too."

"Will do. See you tonight."

CHAPTER FIVE

"How is she?" Meera asked Ailsa.

"Hunter and Tim need to find this monster. Even the look of her wounds was grim. It was as if her eyeballs had been removed with a kitchen knife or something. So much force was used that her left eye socket is broken too. She must have been heavily sedated."

Meera grimaced. She was sure the sight of the young woman sprawled on the bloody floor of the lift would never leave her.

This was the third woman to have been attacked in this very specific way. However, the other two had been left outside. The first in Ravelston Wood. She had been found by a dog walker who was traumatised by the wounds the woman had suffered. Meera had done the post-mortem examination and thought the victim had probably been found two or three days after she had been attacked. Meera was appalled by the brutality that had been inflicted on her.

The second woman was still in one of her freezers. She had been found by a couple of detectorists walking along the beach at Cramond. Meera guessed they were hoping to find Roman coins but thought it more likely they had unearthed beer bottle tops and tin cans. A corpse was certainly not amongst the items they had hoped to find, and both had to be treated for shock. Meera wondered if they would ever enjoy their hobby again.

"Meera, Meera, are you all right?" Ailsa asked.

"Yes, sorry, of course. What did you do for the woman?"

"Her blood pressure was low. She had clearly lost a lot of blood and her body would be in shock too."

"Of course."

"You know, I worked in King's College Hospital A & E in London for years and saw all kinds of wicked attacks, stabbings, beatings and gunshot wounds, but none was callous as this one. We had to put her on blood infusions and fluids while she was waiting for surgery."

"It's horrendous. Did she regain consciousness at all?"

"Not for long. But she told us her name is Eileen Maguire. She asked where 'Frederick' was and why everything was dark."

"God. She muttered the name Frederick to me when she was in the lift."

"What did you tell her. We body swerved the question about Frederick, although I'll tell Hunter of course."

"Hmm. I doubt that'll be Frederick's real name."

"Me too, Meera, but it's all we've got. We told her she'd suffered an injury and was in the Royal Infirmary of Edinburgh. I said she'd have to go for surgery and then she began to cry. It was awful. She still has her tear ducts, and her cheeks got all wet. I've never seen anything like this before."

"No, neither have I. It's horrendous."

"I asked her who her next of kin was. She mentioned her siter Linda."

"Linda Maguire? That name sounds familiar, but I can't remember why," Meera said.

"Anyway, at that point the surgeon came down and instructed us to anesthetise her so that they could carry out their examinations without causing her any further pain or stress."

"She'll have enough of that when she finds out what was done to her."

Meera looked quizzically at Ailsa for a moment. "I think I've remembered who Linda Maguire is, if it's the same person. I think she's Jamie Thomson's girlfriend."

"Oh no. Meera, leave it with me, I'll phone Tim and ask him to contact Jamie and Linda, but to be subtle, in case it's a different girl with the same name."

CHAPTER SIX

Tim accepted another bacon roll from Bear. He started to munch it and drink the last of his coffee then turned to face Hunter who was standing at the front of the room. He hoped his boss felt better than he looked. A grey suit, grey face and greying stubble was not a good look. Hunter's tie hung limply to one side and clearly it would take more than his signature strong, black coffee to bring him fully to this morning's task in hand.

He looked at Rachael when Hunter walked towards her. She shook her head, but it was clear that whatever the boss was asking of her, he wasn't taking no for an answer. He saw her point towards Mel. Hunter shrugged and then nodded. Clearly a compromise had been reached.

Tim watched Hunter walk back towards his original place and heard him ask for the team's attention more quietly than ever before. It was going to be a long day.

"Bear, Tim, if you could stop eating your breakfast for long enough to pay attention to what I have to say, that would be great."

The big men at the back of the room exchanged glances and devoured the remaining food quickly avoiding any waste.

"You promoted yet?" Bear asked Tim.

"Not even sat the exam yet."

"Is the boss's promotion through?"

"No announcement that I know of."

"Would the two of you like to take this briefing? You seem to have a lot to say."

"Sorry, boss," they muttered.

"With DCI Mackay now working with MIT, I'm acting DCI," Hunter said. "Catching the eye thief has become my own circle of hell. I plan to second Neil Larkin to our team because we've lost DC Angus McKenzie to MIT and I want a full complement to catch this bastard fast."

"Charlie won't be pleased, boss," Mel said.

"I will spend the appropriate number of my waking hours worrying about that, DC Grant."

Mel blushed. Tim saw Bear put a hand on her shoulder. When was he going to do the decent thing by her and marry Mel, or at least announce their engagement?

"So, who's going to pretend to be you, if you're being DCI Mackay, boss?"

"Don't be an arse, Bear. I am not pretending to be anybody else. You're working under my rules now. Anyway, I believe a DI is being assigned to us, but who knows when. Tim when is your sergeant's exam?"

"Not heard yet, boss."

"It would make my life a hell of a lot easier if you accepted being fast-tracked young Myerscough."

"Possibly yours, but not mine, boss. I want to get promoted on merit. I don't want anybody to be able to say that I got a promotion because Dad was Chief Constable. I want them to know that I got it because I jumped through all the same hoops as everybody else." Tim looked at Hunter and heard the man sigh, but they both knew he was not going to shift his ground.

"Let's get on then." Hunter said and explained how he and Meera happened to be at the Waldorf Astoria the previous evening and found the injured woman. The team knew about the two women who had been found dead with similar injuries.

"Do we know if the perpetrator is the same person?" DC Nadia Chan asked.

"It's surely likely, because we never revealed that the eyes had been removed from the other corpses," DS Colin Reid said.

"How come this one didn't die?" Bear asked.

"Her name is Eileen Maguire, Bear. I suspect the only reason she's alive is that Meera and I found her shortly after the attack and the ambulance got her to hospital quickly. She got fluids and blood to stabilise her blood pressure and the Accident and Emergency Team managed the shock and kept her alive."

"But she's still blind?"

"She has no eyes, Bear. Of course, she's blind." Hunter shook his head. "Tim, when Eileen was asked who her next of kin is, she mentioned a sister, Linda."

"Shit. Linda Maguire is Jamie Thomson's girlfriend. I got some rambling message from Ailsa yesterday. That must be what she was trying to tell me."

"It may not be the same Linda Maguire, but can you contact Jamie and Linda to find out if it's possible?"

"Bloody hell, how do I introduce that into a conversation?"

"You'll find a way, lad. Now, uniforms went round the staff

in the reception, bar and Pompadour Restaurant to try to get details of the man Eileen was with. She seemed to think his name was Frederick, but I doubt that's going to be true."

"No chance," DS Colin Reid said.

"I agree, Colin. They did manage to get descriptions from four members of staff. They're all different. Of course, I can't really criticise, as I was sitting facing Meera and wasn't aware of Eileen's table at all. Still, I will file a witness report this morning."

"Should you be involved in the case, I mean if you're a witness, boss?" Colin asked.

"Are you volunteering to lead the team, DS Reid?"

"No boss."

"I want all the witnesses to go through our mugshots and see if they recognise anybody. Also, our newly qualified victim support officer, DC Anderson, is assigned to our victim when she is sufficiently recovered. Right Rachael?"

"Yes, boss."

CHAPTER
SEVEN

"Don't you think that sounds a bit mean, Jamie? I mean, the Morrisons have never done anything nasty to us."

"You're soft, Linda. And anyway, they've been talking out of turn about Frankie's twins."

"No, surely not! They're only little girls."

"Don't let them hear you say that. They think they're big girls now. Let's get a cuppa tea and I'll tell you all about Pop's plan."

Jamie followed her into the kitchen and stood and watched her fill the kettle, take two teabags out of the cupboard, the milk out of the fridge and add three teaspoons of sugar to his mug.

"You should really take less sugar, you know."

"Yes, I know. Shall we have a couple of biscuits?" Jamie reached for the tin. He saw her smile at him. He thought Linda could really be the one.

"I wonder how Eileen's date went last night. She was excited. Frederick, I think she said the guy's name was."

"They met online if I remember. Very dodgy if you ask me."

"Well, I didn't. She had talked to him for ages, first online, then on the phone, then facetime."

"Yeh, yeh. I know. Hob nob or chocolate digestive?"

"Chocolate every time. And he was taking her to that fancy restaurant in the Waldorf Astoria. It's a very public place. Nothing could go wrong there."

"Where's the Waldorf Astoria then?" He picked up the biscuits and followed her back to the living room.

"You know, it used to be The Caledonian at the west end of Princes Street."

"Aye, well, it may surprise you to know that is not one of my usual haunts," he said. "Cuddle up and I'll tell you pop's plan while Frankie and Donna are out."

They sat close together on the sofa and Jamie mentioned how his pop wanted a room when he was released from prison, but Ian thought the house would be much too crowded.

"That's true, we've already got all three bedrooms taken with Frankie and Donna in the big room, you and me in the second and then Kylie and Dannii in the wee room. Your pop would have to sleep in the bath," Linda said.

"Exactly what he thought, so he suggested we move out. After all, this is really Frankie's house. Pop doesn't want to go far because he likes to look out for Frankie."

"From the big house?"

"Aye, well. You know what I mean."

Jamie reached for a biscuit and explained that his pop had heard the Morrisons in the other half of their semi-detached house planned to move and suggested that Jamie make life a bit uncomfortable for them, so they went sooner rather than later. That way they'd be away by the time pop was out on parole and needed a room. He smiled and told her that pop thought the nuisance he would cause should also make sure the Morrisons were willing to accept a quick sale and a lower price.

"How does your pop know that they even want to move, Jamie. I mean, he's inside."

"Pop's got his contacts. Nowt much gets past him."

Jamie heard his phone ring and walked back through to the kitchen where he'd left it. Why was a copper calling him? He hadn't even done anything yet.

"Blondie, need a new car?" He asked Tim hopefully.

"Not this time, Jamie. Is Linda about?"

"Aye. Linda it's Tim. Here she is."

"No Jamie, I don't want to speak to Linda. I need you to move to where she can't overhear us."

"Hang on, let me check the motor." When Jamie was seated in the front of his car, he pretended to rummage around in the glove compartment. "Okay, Tim I'm in the car and she's still in the house. What's up?"

"Is it possible that Linda's sister was having dinner at The Pompadour Restaurant of the Waldorf Astoria last night?"

"Is that the really posh place, used to be The Caledonian or what?"

"Yes. Expensive too."

"Yep, she was there on a first date with this guy she met online. I think all that's dodgy, but Linda says no, Eileen was really careful and went slowly, slowly to get to know him. Then of course, they meet first in a public place, so she's fine."

"Have you heard from her?"

"No. Why?"

"Was her date's name Frederick by any chance?"

"Yes. Look, how come you're so interested in Eileen's love life? You've got a bird."

"I don't think Eileen is fine, Jamie. A young woman called Eileen Maguire, who's sister is Linda was attacked last night. We think the attack was carried out by her date, whose name was Frederick."

"Fuck. Don't tell me she's dead. I can't tell Linda her sister is dead. What happened, Tim."

"I don't know all the details, but she's in an induced coma in intensive care at the Royal Infirmary. Do you want me to pick you and Linda up?"

"No, I'll drive it'll be faster."

"I can blues and twos and you'll not have to park. I can be with you in fifteen minutes."

"Right. Fine. Fucking hell, Tim, what do I tell Linda?"

CHAPTER EIGHT

Meera and her colleague, David Murray, were the attending pathologists.

"Did I tell you Chrissie and I are expecting?"

"Again? How many will this be?" Meera asked.

"Six. I'm hoping to make it to a football team." David grinned as he washed his hands.

"I can just hear Chrissie's views on that, Dr Murray," Meera said.

She scrubbed up and disinfected her hands then made her way over to the examination room where David was already waiting for her. He had wheeled in the body of the second victim into the hospital mortuary. Meera looked around her domain and thought how much her post-mortem examination room looked like an operating theatre.

David had already transferred the corpse to a stainless-steel table that occupied the middle of the spotlessly clean white floor. The victim was lying on her back with her arms loosely resting by her sides. Meera glanced at David and shook her head.

"This is so vicious," she said. "And very difficult when we know so little about the victim."

"That's true. But we'll find out what we can. Who do you think will attend for Police Scotland today?"

"I believe detectorists found the corpse in its original site on Cramond beach and PC Neil Larkin was the first officer on the scene. Hunter told me that he planned to second Neil to CID, so I believe he and Nadia Chan have been delegated to come today."

"Well, I hope Neil manages a little better than some of the other first timers. Didn't Bear Zewedu faint during his first post-mortem?"

Meera nodded.

"But Nadia is a trouper. We can always rely on her, at least to stay conscious." David smiled.

Meera turned her attention to the body on the table. She noted the livor mortis on the woman's body caused by the settling of the blood.

"She was definitely not killed in the location where she was found." David frowned.

"True enough indeed. Oh, it sounds like the boys and girls in blue are arriving," Meera said.

As Neil and Nadia walked towards the examination room, Meera looked up and smiled.

"DC Chan, how good to see you again."

"Thanks Doctor Sharma. This is my colleague DC Larkin."

"DC Larkin, hello. Thank you for coming. It seems we were correct on

our guess of attending officers, David."

"Post mortems are always interesting, but I would happily never come here again if it meant that people stopped getting killed," Nadia looked at the Meera then at Neil.

"And I would just quite happily never come here again. It smells awful."

"We should get gowned up, Neil," Nadia said. "This way."

"There really is a distinctive smell in here, isn't there?" Neil commented as he followed Nadia.

"Yes, a bit like a combination of formaldehyde, antiseptic and industrial soap, isn't it? It's also a bit chilly, just those few degrees below what would be considered comfortable makes all the difference."

When Nadia and Neil returned to witness the post-mortem, Neil said, "It's a big room."

"Yes, well by the time I've got my large double sinks along the wall, a metal counter to hold all the tools and the channel leading to the drain, I suppose it has to be big," Meera said.

"When you two are finished discussing the equipment, might we get on with the job?" David asked.

The two DCs moved so that they could see the body on the stainless-steel examination table below the powerful circular halogen lights which were suspended from the ceiling. Meera positioned herself on the other side of the table from the two detectives. They watched in silence as Meera first freed the body from its sandy, laced shoes. There were cuts and grazes on the body's hands possibly from a fight she put up against her attacker and there were animal bites and scratches that she had suffered since death. Meera also noticed the tiny abrasions and colour changes around the neck.

"David, look at this," Meera said. "Her neck was bound, held or restrained in some way, by the looks of things. She might have been throttled into unconsciousness before her eyes were removed."

David pulled a face as he watched Meera remove the clothes from the top of the body to get a better look. "There's bits of sand and dirt stuck to that," he said. "Probably from after she was dumped on the beach."

"Yes, that would be right. She was just above the tideline when the metal detecting guys called it in. That's where I first saw her," Neil said.

As each piece of clothing was taken from the body, Meera methodically gave them to David. He put each item carefully into plastic evidence bags which would be handed over to the forensics experts for further examination. Meera then took blood, urine and hair samples as well as oral and anal swabs. Meera removed the victim's underwear – the first thing she noticed was the large bruise on the victim's belly.

"Look at this, David," she said. "I wouldn't be surprised if he knelt on her to get the purchase to remove the eyes. We'll need to check for injuries to the internal organs."

"Nasty!" David Murray frowned.

"I don't suppose there's much doubt about the cause of death." Neil grimaced.

"I don't like to pre-empt our findings, but the poor soul would have suffered severe shock from the removal of the eyeballs and if we find damage to the internal organs, there could be massive internal bleeding inside the abdominal cavity," Meera said.

Then David looked at Neil. "We expect to find evidence that she was drugged like the first victim. If so, she would never have recovered consciousness from that and the strangulation. The victims may not even have felt the pain from the cut."

Nadia gasped. Neil closed his eyes and fell to the floor with a thud.

"And he was doing so well," David said.

Nadia said nothing. She just placed Neil gently into the recovery position, apologised to the doctors and invited them to continue with their work.

David nodded and reached for the digital camera. He documented everything as Meera finished undressing the body. She scraped gently underneath the nails of each of the fingers.

"I've got fragments of skin here that might give us DNA from the attacker," she said.

She then sprayed the body with fungicide and used a hose with a powerful water jet to methodically wash and disinfect the corpse fully. When she was finished, she turned on her voice recorder and dictated the official examination.

She began by stating the date and time, followed by the case number then she described the general state of the body, before she moved on to describe the grisly details. Meera checked that the directional light in her headset was switched on, although she knew it was, it gave her a couple of seconds to compose herself discreetly before she began checking the skin around the corpse's neck.

"No other suspicious bruises," David commented.

A touch check of the neck revealed that both the larynx and trachea of the victim had collapsed.

"And her hyoid bone in the neck is fractured, so it suggests that she was strangled probably before the eyes were removed. The strangulation could have been used to subdue or maybe to move her," Meera said glancing at David.

"There was no sign of anything that might have been used to strangle her when the body was found, was there?" Meera asked Nadia.

"Not that I know of. Neil could better answer that if he were awake. Do you want me to give him a shake?"

"No, just leave him, Nadia." Meera then turned her attention back to the body. She checked for signs of sexual or any other kind of aggression. She began with the mouth: pulling it open and checking for any trauma or skin and teeth colour alteration in case a poison had been used that discoloured the teeth or tongue or perhaps burned the skin inside her mouth. Meera found no primary indications of poisoning, but samples would be sent for a toxicology report in any event.

"Hunter and I came across a young woman yesterday who had suffered a similar attack. I think there were about six months between the first victim and this woman, but if it is the same attacker there are only a few weeks between this victim and the woman we found." Meera sighed.

"That would be very worrying. You must find this monster DC Chan," David said.

Nadia jumped into the driver's seat and Neil crawled into the passenger seat beside her.

"How long was I out for?"

"Just over an hour. Don't worry, it happens a lot. I think the boss was late for a darts match and he was furious."

"That doesn't make me feel any better."

Nadia manoeuvred around the carpark. With a quick glance around her and up at the tall black buildings that formed the canyon that is the Cowgate, then she pulled into the flow of traffic.

"Will you say happened with me?" Neil asked.

"Of course." She smiled and headed back to the station.

CHAPTER NINE

Tim pulled up in front of the Accident and Emergency department of the hospital building.

"She's in intensive care now, but my sister admitted Eileen when she first came in and she wants to speak to you before you see her."

"That the one I've met?"

"Probably, I only have one sister."

Jamie nodded and went towards the automatic doors side by side with Linda. He heard Tim slam the car door shut and drive off. There were never enough parking spaces at the hospital.

He looked around the department and caught sight of Ailsa Myerscough. Even in sensible, flat shoes, Ailsa was taller than most people around her. Of course, Blondie was right tall too. Jamie saw she was deep in conversation with a colleague, but then she caught sight of them. As soon as she did, she appeared to finish up what she was saying. Jamie watched her colleague turn to look at them, grimace then nod while Ailsa sped towards them.

"Hello, Jamie. And you must be Linda, Eileen's sister." She shook their hands. "Follow me, and we'll go into the relatives room. Would you prefer tea or coffee?" she asked.

"Tea, Ailsa." Jamie muttered.

She made the sign of a letter T towards the colleague she had been speaking to. Then moved towards a door halfway down the right-hand wall. She sat down and motioned for them to use the chairs on the other side of a low coffee table.

"I know Eileen's poorly. She's been attacked by that bastard who took her out, hasn't she? But she's going to be okay, isn't she? I mean, they gave her an operation to make everything okay again, didn't they? I mean it's good you were here when she arrived, wasn't it?" Linda rambled.

There was a soft knock on the door and a nurse brought in three mugs of tea, some little cartons of UHT milk, a few sachets of sugar and some wooden sticks to stir with. Jamie noticed there were biscuits on a plate too, but no chocolate ones.

Linda continued to talk. "She must have been hurt bad because we don't normally get tea and biscuits anywhere. That's for posh folks, isn't it? So, when will Eileen get home? Will she have to stay with us for a few days or can she go back to her flat? She lives alone, you see."

Jamie caught the look in Ailsa's eyes. This was not going to be good news. *Oh God. Just stop talking Linda.*

"Help yourselves to milk and sugar," Ailsa said. Then she offered them each a biscuit. "I don't know exactly what happened to Eileen, but I'll tell you what I know and then I'll take you up to the ICU and you can see her."

Jamie listened to Ailsa as she explained that Eileen had been found by a police detective and a doctor on the floor of a lift in the fancy hotel. Jamie remembered casing the same place some years ago with his pop. It had a different name then. He seemed to remember that they did okay out of it. He realised he had stopped hearing what Ailsa was saying. He looked at Linda. She had turned white. The undigested tea and biscuits reappeared from her mouth and splashed all over the coffee table.

She shook uncontrollably. Tears were streaming down her face. He saw her coat covered in vomit. Oh God. Jamie stared at Ailsa. What had he missed?

"So just now she's blind? What are they going to do about it? Who would do such a horrible thing? Take her whole eyeball out? That's disgusting." Linda shouted.

Jamie's lip curled inadvertently. He felt the bile rise in his gullet. Fucking hell why would anybody do that? He swallowed the sour taste. It took two or three goes to get the sick sensation out of his mouth. He tried to clear his throat but his voice only came out in a whisper.

"Sorry, doc. What happened exactly?"

"Both Eileen's eyeballs have been removed from their sockets on her face. I believe she was probably drugged, although I haven't seen the blood reports, they went up to the ward. Still, I can't imagine anybody being able to stand the pain and shock of such an attack if they were conscious."

"What have they done? Have they put new eyes in or her eyes back or what?"

"Jamie, we can't do that. Going forward, Eileen's life will be that of a blind person."

"Fucking shit, Ailsa. Who did this? By Christ they're going to suffer."

"I don't know who did it, Jamie. That's a police matter. Had she not been found so soon after the attack, I don't believe she would have survived. When she came into hospital her body was in shock and she had lost a great deal of blood. Once we stabilised her condition, she was taken to the theatre. Her wounds were cleaned out and the blood vessels and nerve endings repaired as far as possible so that they don't cause her more pain and have less chance of becoming infected."

"This is grim," Jamie said. "She'll move in with us, of course." He looked at Linda.

"I'll have to look after her," Linda said.

"Blind people can lead independent lives, you know. Don't make plans for Eileen without discussing her wishes although, of course, her rehabilitation will take a long time."

Jamie looked across at Ailsa. His expression had turned from one of horror to fury. "It was that bastard that took her out, wasn't it? Groomed her and then stole her fucking eyes. Frederick, you said his name was, Linda."

"I don't know who it did, but I have no doubt the police are working on it as we speak," Ailsa said. "Eileen is still in an induced coma, but would you like to come up and see her now?"

I didn't really want to see her again, but I was curious to see my handiwork. I told them at reception I was her brother, and they gave me the ward number, no questions asked.

It was when I was going along the corridor, I realised there was a doctor and a couple talking about Eileen. They must be going to see her. Probably her sister and the dodgy guy she goes out with. I didn't want to meet them. His dad's in Saughton and hard by all accounts.

I patted myself down, as if I'd forgotten something and turned to leave. I took the stairs rather than the lift. Less chance of meeting anybody else. I'll stop by another time.

CHAPTER TEN

"Good of the boss to let us all away to go to this," Tim said.

"Not really, we're both on a day off and you only got time off because your ex is Lady Dalmore," Bear said. He held Mel's hand as she climbed out of the back of Tim's big BMW.

Tim looked back and pressed his key fob to check his car was locked. He caught sight of Simon Land striding towards them with his brother Robin by his side. They all shook hands.

"Look they're going in. Let's make sure we get a seat. This will be a busy funeral." Mel said.

"I'll have a seat, whatever happens," Robin said.

"Always the pragmatist." Tim smiled at her and led the way.

"Where's Gillian?" Simon asked Tim.

"She's packing. She's determined to take a job she's been offered at the Moscow State University."

"I don't blame her. That's an incredible opportunity," Robin said. "But will she be safe?"

Tim shrugged. "She says so and respected as a Professor at the university." They fell silent as they stepped inside. He looked around and recognised many of the great and the good of Edinburgh's legal society. Members of the nobility were there along with the political figures of Scotland. Tim knew most of the politicians, at least by sight. They had served with his father in the Scottish Parliament, but none of them would confess to knowing him now. Even a minor royal had been despatched to pay respects. Everyone was looking around to check who else was there and making sure their own presence was noted. Reading and re-reading the order of service, they glanced up only to nod acknowledgements to those they felt were their social equals or superiors.

Tim didn't bother, but nor did he hide. At six feet four inches tall and sitting beside the only black man in the room, that would have been impossible. He smiled. He knew his wealth was greater than most of the dignitaries present. He also knew few of them considered him their social equal and would have laughed if he had claimed otherwise, despite the fact he went to Merchiston Castle School and graduated with First Class honours from St. Andrews University.

It was a shame. Lord Dalmore died so young. He had been a decent man. Tim enjoyed knowing him. He got to know him well over the years that he had dated his daughter, Sophie. Tim never told him why he ended that relationship. He doubted Sophie ever did either.

More people entered. Tim understood that Lord Dalmore had been proud of his heritage and the law firm his family had established, but the man Tim knew was quiet and thoughtful. He couldn't help wondering how the new Lord Dalmore, Sophie's brother Geoffrey, would be like as head of the family.

Tim missed Gillian's presence. When he glanced over at Bear and Mel, he noticed that they sat closely together and whispered quietly. Simon sat at the end of the row behind them so that Robin in his wheelchair was beside him.

The minister asked the congregation to stand if they could as the coffin was brought to the front of the gathering. As Tim did so, he felt a hollowness in the core of his being. One of the good men of the city had passed. Tim would miss him; his calm influence and incisive intellect would be a great loss to those who knew him.

The family followed the coffin. Geoffrey limped with his peculiar gait and held onto his mother. Lady Dalmore wept openly, and it was impossible for Tim to work out which of them was supporting the other. Sophie walked behind them. She was dressed in a chic, black, embroidered dress coat. God she was gorgeous. She looked up and smiled directly at him. She still made him stiff. Bugger.

The service took almost an hour, largely because of a verbose eulogy given by the Dean of the Faculty of Advocates. That man had always liked the sound of his own voice.

The congregation stood again as the family walked towards the door and stood in line to shake hands with those who had paid their respects. However, Geoffrey's short arms and misshapen hands were withered and not well suited for shaking, Lady Dalmore was unsuccessful in containing her grief and therefore the bulk of the glad handing fell to Sophie. Tim watched her smile as she charmed each individual in turn.

He decided to avoid a potentially embarrassing encounter, so he moved aside and gathered with his friends without joining the line. They discussed the service and the length of the eulogy. Why did everybody choose the hymn Abide with Me and psalm 23 The Lord's My Shepherd?

"I wonder how Geoffrey will cope with his father's title,"

Bear said. "He's intelligent, but his mobility's not great and he needs help with basic care."

"Excuse me. Disabled farmer in the group," Robin said.

"True, but nobody ever said you were intelligent." Bear joked.

"Fuck off, Zewedu."

Tim watched Sophie walk towards them. He held out his hand and offered her his condolences.

She ignored his hand and took him into her arms. "Oh Tim, I'm so glad you're here. It's been so awful. Mum is a basket case and Geoffrey is even more of a prig than usual. He expects me to give up our flat and my job and move back to help him run the estate."

"I'm sure he will need help, but are you the right person to give it? He probably needs to sit down with your dad's accountant and estate manager before he takes any decisions."

"I'd advise against doing anything life changing so soon after your father's death," Simon said. "When our dad died and Robin and I took over the farm, it was months before we sorted all the legalities and worked out our respective roles."

"And dad's farm was much smaller than your family estate," Robin said.

"Will you or Geoffrey go back into your family legal firm?" Tim asked.

"I really don't know. I can't think," Sophie said.

Tim was glad to see the tears in her eyes. It made her look more humane to him.

"You will all come to the wake, won't you?"

"Sorry, Sophie, Robin and I have to get back to the farm. Too close to lambing for us to skive."

"Mel and I are getting a lift back with Tim, sorry." Bear said.

"But Timmy, you'll stay. Please stay and hold my hand."

"With the best will in the world, that's no longer my place, Sophe. Anyway, once I've got these good people safely back to Marchmont, I have to make an emergency mission to pick up Lucky from rehab."

"I didn't think he got out till tomorrow."

Tim blushed. He had always been a rotten liar. "I got an SOS call from him because his cousin Felix has gone AWOL, apparently and the rehab unit won't let Lucky out unaccompanied. I have to take him home and wait with him until the person has come out to put on his tag for the home detention curfew."

"I don't envy you that," Sophie said. "I suppose I'll have to put up with my mother and the new Lord Dalmore all alone. Thank you all for coming. I better find the car to take me to the hotel."

Tim watched her move towards those who would take up her offer of hospitality.

"She still does it for you, doesn't she Tim?" Mel asked.

"Let's go. I'm going to crash with you for the afternoon."

"I thought you had to rescue Lucky."

"Tomorrow. Sophie was right. I just can't go and smile and be nice to people. It's exhausting at the best of times, and this is not one of them. Shall we go to The Golf Tavern or stay back at yours?"

"Either sounds good to me. Simon, Robin, see you soon," Bear said and then followed Tim as he turned and strode towards the car.

"Will Gillian join us?" Mel asked.

"Probably, if she can fit us into her busy schedule."

CHAPTER
ELEVEN

"Right pipe down you lot," Hunter said. "Let's officially welcome DC Neil Larkin to CID." He waited for the round of applause and stomping feet to quieten. "First round's on you, Neil."

"Drinks, drinks," Bear shouted.

"Now back to business. Forensics got some fingerprints in the blood on the walls of the elevator. Unfortunately, only mine and Meera's came up. We're both on the elimination database."

"We have another clear thumb print and a middle and index finger, but not on record. So, they're no use to us until we've found our man." He paused and looked around the room. Then he continued to speak. "On the bright side the descriptions from staff at the hotel and other guests in the bar and dining room have allowed us to get a general idea of what our perpetrator looks like."

"Good," Neil said.

"Yep, except that there are four different photofits of him."

"Bloody hell," Colin said. "Can we not just get a break boss?"

Hunter taped the four pictures onto the white board.

"That first one is a dead ringer for Arjun Mansoor," Mel said. "But he's still in Saughton Prison, I think."

"We'll need to find out from HMP Edinburgh if there's any chance he was outside the walls at the time the attack took place," Hunter said.

"Don't you think that second one could be Lucky, or Lord Lachlan Buchanan as he's known to his friends, Tim?" Bear asked.

"Could be, or it could be his cousin Felix. The eyes are a bit too close together for Lucky."

"I see what you mean, yes."

"That third one is John Hamilton to a tee. Look, they've even got his big, fat nose," Colin said.

"If I remember correctly, John Hamilton has big, fat everything," Nadia said. "And I hate to say it boss, but that bottom picture could be you, if you'd forgotten to shave."

"Everyone loves a comedian, Nadia."

"No, boss, she's right," Colin said.

"Okay, Colin, you and Nadia down to the hotel and check over the CCTV. Let's see if we've caught our man in glorious technicolour."

Colin and Nadia exchanged glances. They knew they were good at the detailed work required when reviewing CCTV.

"Bear, you and Neil make the necessary enquiries and establish the whereabouts of Mansoor, Lucky, Felix and Hamilton on the night in question. Rachael, now that you've finished your Victim Support training, I'm assigning your first victim to you. You will be there for Miss Eileen Maguire and look after her and her family."

"God, that's a baptism of fire, boss," Mel said.

"Yes, that's why you will go with Rachael to speak to the victim's sister, today. I understand that the victim is still in an induced coma, but find out what the family knows, will you?"

"That'll be a little slice of heaven for you, Mel. Her other half is Jamie Thomson," Tim said.

"Don't I know it!"

"Ah yes, Tim. Take our mugshot books down to the hotel and see if any of the staff recognise the perpetrator from any of the photos on file."

"Sure, boss. You remember I'm off early today. I have to pick up Lucky from rehab."

"I know. But fuck's sake young Myerscough, you've got almost seven hours between now and then. Get on with it."

CHAPTER TWELVE

Eileen knew she wasn't awake, but she could hear Linda. Her sister was sobbing and crying and kept screaming at that chump she's going out with. She was asking him what kind of fiend would steal someone's eyes. Eileen thought Linda must have had too much to drink. Why were they in her flat when she was trying to sleep? It was a funny kind of sleep; she couldn't open her eyes to see them.

The chump tried to soothe her, but she was having none of it. She gets like that when she's had a few. She should get rid of him anyway, after all his father was nothing short of a gangster.

Eileen tried to work out why her flat smelt of disinfectant. Had Linda been cleaning? Why couldn't her sister just mind her own business? She seems to be saying Eileen can't manage. True, I don't feel up to much right now, but it'll be fine when I've had a bit of sleep, if she'd just shut up.

It's dark in here. Darker than she remembers. Then she thinks she must have ordered those blackout blinds she was thinking about. She likes a dark room when she's sleeping and there are so many streetlights in the roads near her flat.

Then she thinks about Frederick and hopes he found his way home safely. What a lovely meal he treated her to, but she doesn't remember saying goodbye. She hopes she wasn't rude and that he'll take her out again.

He didn't look quite like his picture, but that didn't matter one bit. It made no difference at all. He called her darling. He was the only man who'd ever called her darling.

CHAPTER THIRTEEN

RACHEL SLID INTO THE PASSENGER SEAT OF THE CAR. SHE WAS GLAD Mel was driving to the hospital. Why had she ever volunteered to become a victim support officer? And now she had a traumatised blind woman as her first case. At least the woman was still in a coma, so she wouldn't have to deal with the woman's fear today. And the bloody brother-in-law was Jamie Thomson. That guy was a maniac. Mel could deal with him.

Gosh, they were already at the hospital. Her mind had wandered for the whole journey. And Mel got a parking space. This woman led a charmed life.

"Shall we go in and see Ailsa first? She was the admitting doctor when Eileen arrived?" Mel asked.

"It can't do any harm, can it? At least she could give us the background." Rachael followed Mel into A&E so closely that she almost walked into her when Mel stopped to speak to the medic.

"...I heard from her consultant they plan to start waking her up today," Ailsa said. "The shorter the time she's in a coma, the better."

"Better for whom?" Rachael said. Then realised she had spoken.

"The patient of course. And they'll have to tell her about her injuries and how life will change going forward. It will be hard for her to take in. She'll need a great deal of support and love from family and friends."

"I just hope the bold Jamie will step up," Mel said. "Which ward is she in?"

"Still in ICU, I imagine because they'll be keeping a close watch on her respiration and circulation. Especially with that kind of injury. She's had surgery to her eye sockets and the blood supply around that part of her face, so her circulation is a matter of particular concern."

"Will we even be allowed in?" Rachael asked.

"You might be. But, even if she's awake you won't be allowed to ask any delving questions, I don't think. Ask the nurse in charge. She'll tell you how Eileen is and whether you can go in."

"Thanks, Ailsa. Which way is it?" Mel asked.

"Go along that corridor, the lift is on the right-hand side about halfway along."

Rachael followed Mel along to the lifts. "My stomach is churning. I think I'm going to be sick, Mel" Rachael said.

"No, you're not. Don't be such a woose."

They walked towards intensive care. Rachael's steps got smaller and smaller as she dragged further behind Mel.

"Come on. Shape up, woman. It's not you who's lost body parts." Mel spoke briefly to the nurse in charge, then turned back to Rachael. "She's awake. The doctors are in with her now explaining her injuries and what they had to do. We'll have to wait until they're finished. My guess is it'll take a while. Shall we just sit here?"

Rachael and Mel sat down on two of the cheap plastic chairs in the corridor and looked sadly into the ICU that housed Eileen Maguire. The doctor spoke softly, but they could hear Eileen sobbing. Who could blame her?

"I'll never see again?" She screamed hysterically.

"When he said I had beautiful eyes and he wanted them for his own, I thought that meant having the rest of me too. I never thought of this. What am I going to do? Frederick said he loved me and called me 'darling'. How could he do this to me? Why would he be so cruel? How will I manage? I won't even be able to see the kettle to make a cup of tea."

"You'll be amazed at what you can do," the doctor said. "But you will have to relearn some things. There are amazing aides and gadgets. You'll certainly be able to make tea."

The detectives watched as Eileen began sobbing.

"Bloody hell, she still cries real tears," Rachael said.

They didn't know how long they'd been sitting in the corridor.

"My bum's gone numb," Mel said.

"Lucky you, I can still feel mine. Do you think they'll let us in soon?"

"They said to give Eileen some time before they tell her we're here. Do you think she's had long enough?"

"Here comes the head nurse, let's ask."

After some discussion the nurse said, "let me tell her you're here and ask if she feels ready to have a short discussion with you. However, if she becomes upset or stressed, I'll have to ask you to leave." She went in and spoke to Eileen and waved them in. "Ten minutes, and no stress. I mean it."

Mel introduced them both and Eileen asked them to sit on opposite sides of the bed and tell her who was speaking.

"I suppose I'll need to get used to listening to people's voices more carefully now that I can't bloody see. Who would do something this ghastly?" She asked and began to cry again. "And who's looking after Princess Leia?"

"Eileen, I'm Rachael, DC Anderson. Please don't cry. Who is Princess Leia?" Rachael asked.

"My cat." Eileen almost screamed the words.

"I'll check, but I'm sure Linda and Jamie have that sorted."

"Then it'll be the first time Jamie's ever got anything sorted without a hitch."

Mel chuckled. "I understand what you mean. But I think he is doing his best for you and Linda."

"Who said that?"

"Sorry, it's Mel, DC Grant. We don't know that it was your date who attacked you, but it does seem likely. You're really very lucky, we believe the same person assaulted two other women, but they didn't get help fast enough. Both of those victims died."

"Well seen you've still got your eyes. I'm the lucky one, am I? Excuse me if I don't feel too bloody lucky right now. And if it wasn't Frederick who assaulted me, who the hell do you think it was? Did someone else just happen to get into the lift of the posh hotel with me and cut out my eyes? I may be blind, but I'm not stupid. It has to have been him. We were alone when we got into the lift, then I must have passed out. I don't remember anything else."

"You're probably right, but we have to keep our avenues of investigation as wide as possible. We don't want any more women suffering similar attacks."

"Remember to tell me your name. It's not much to ask," Eileen said.

"Of course not, I'm sorry."

"You did it again."

"Sorry, I'm Rachael. Can you tell me how you and Frederick met?"

"A friend at work fixed me up with an account for a dating website. That's where we met. Sounds pathetic, doesn't it? I should've been able to get a boyfriend through folk I know, but it hadn't happened. I was lonely."

"Mel here, Eileen. No, it doesn't sound pathetic, Eileen. Lots of couples meet online now. However you meet anybody, you don't deserve to be attacked."

"Not just attacked. He took my fucking eyes. Who does that? Who even thinks like that? I'm blind for the rest of my life." She began to cry again and the tears from behind the bandages were hard to watch.

"I'm Rachael. Eileen, you're blind now, but you weren't when you met this guy. And you are our best hope of catching him and locking him up. You can help us stop him hurting anyone else's like this, if you feel strong enough. Will you help us?"

"Damn right I will, if it's the last worthwhile thing I do, I'll help you get this monster. You know the funny thing is, when I met him at The Waldorf Astoria, he didn't look quite the same as when we face timed on the phone."

"Great, Eileen. Tell Mel and me about that."

"The first photo I saw was on the dating website. He took it down when we started talking. He was lying on the beach with his dog, a Labrador, I think. I'm not great at dogs, though. The angle the shot was taken his legs looked extremely long. He seemed tall with dark hair and a bushy beard."

"Eileen, it's Mel here. What colour was his beard?"

"That's a funny question. It was dark brown, maybe black. It depended on the light how dark it looked."

"The reason I asked, I'm still Mel, is that often men with dark hair grow beards that have a reddish hue."

"No. There was never any red in it. On the phone, in the photos or in real life. His beard was dark. Oh, and I can tell your voices apart now. If that helps."

"Thanks Eileen, it does. But that description makes me wonder if his beard was real."

"Wow. I never thought of that. The hair on his arms and legs was dark too and his limbs in the dating website photos were muscular and sexy." She smiled at the memory. It was the first time the detectives had seen her smile.

"What about when you spoke on the phone. What did his limbs look like then?" Rachael asked.

"I never saw them. The camera was always trained onto his face. Of course, so was mine. He wanted to see my eyes, didn't he? He had beautiful big brown eyes. They seemed so kind and loving. What kind of idiot am I?"

"Not idiotic at all. Have you always been this hard on yourself?"

Eileen smiled again. "You know, Rachael, I think I have."

"Eileen, can you think about what he sounded like? What kind of accent did he have?"

"I didn't really notice an accent, Mel. I suppose he must have been local."

"Interesting. Where did he tell you he lived?"

"He said he lived in a big house in North Berwick with his cousin, but who knows. Was everything he told me a lie?" Eileen began to cry again.

The nurse bustled in. "Detectives, I said a few minutes. You have overstayed your welcome and upset my patient."

"Sorry, nurse. Thank you for your help, Eileen. We may need to come back. Will that be okay with you?"

"Yes, Mel. It will be fine. I'll give you all the help I can to track down this devil."

CHAPTER FOURTEEN

The detectives turned to leave and saw Jamie and Linda walking towards them.

"DC Grant," Jamie said. "Always a pleasure to see you. Are you working on Eileen's case? You need to find the bastard before I do, Mel, otherwise I'll be going down for life."

"The whole team is working on this, Jamie. Hellish isn't it?"

"That really doesn't touch the sides. It's fucking unbelievable. She's such a quiet girl, Eileen. She didn't deserve this."

"Nobody would," Rachael said.

"Jamie, if you're going to chat to the police, I'm going in to sit with Eileen. Join us when you're ready."

"Of course, Linda. I just want a quick word with DC Grant."

"Do you have a suspect yet, Mel?" Jamie leant against the wall of the hall away from Eileen's room and angled himself so that Linda couldn't see his face. "How can I help?"

"Jamie, please, I know you're trying to be useful, but just leave it to us. The police is the best agency to work the leads."

"Good you have some leads? That's sound. Who are we looking for?"

"You know I can't tell you that. But you could help by letting me know if you hear anything. Even if Eileen mentions something that might be useful when you're talking."

"Aye. Course I will. You do know she's going to be blind forever? Bloody shocking. She'll have to come and stay with me and Linda."

"Isn't your place a bit crowded already with Frankie and Donna and the twins? How old are the girls now?"

"Three. They're growing fast. Don't worry about us, I've got a plan."

"Why does that sentence fill me with dread? Well, just keep on this side of the law, will you, Jamie?"

"Of course, DC Grant. You know me."

"I know you only too well, that's why I said it."

"I'm hurt. That's not a kind thing to say. No, my plan is one I came up with together with my pop."

"Now that does upset me."

"It's quite simple. And you don't need to worry. He heard the other half of Frankie's semi is due to come up for sale and what with Donna and Frankie being engaged, he thought we should buy the other half of the house. You know, spread us out a bit, so I'll have a bedroom and plenty space for Eileen."

"I'm not sure I want to know the answer to this, but how does your pop, who's tucked away in HMP Edinburgh, know that your neighbours plan to sell their home?"

"Arjun Mansoor mentioned it. He knows them. Anyway, the place isn't quite for sale yet, but it will be soon. Watch this space. What a break, eh?"

"Mel, I don't think you should ask any more questions. We're just going to learn something that we'll have to act on."

"You're right, Rache. Bye Jamie. Take care of Linda and Eileen."

"I will Mel. I'll do just that. Lovely to see you honey. Don't pine for me too much, cos Linda and I are solid."

Mel couldn't help grinning at the young man's cheek as she led the way along the corridor and towards the exit of the hospital.

Of course, it would have been cleaner if this one bled out and died like the others. But the fact that she's still alive is exciting, in a strange way. Maybe now I've found out which hospital she's in, I can watch the result of my work.

Yes, it would be fun to see how she copes with my handiwork. Maybe I can even go in to see her. She won't see me. Now that would be intoxicating.

I also know of Dr Gillian Pearson. She has bright green eyes. Deep, emerald, green. Those would be a fine addition to the collection. Pity she's got Tim Myerscough as her boyfriend, he's a bit overprotective of those in his group. Still, I'm sure I can get round that problem somehow. She's certainly not difficult to spot, with that bright green flash in her hair.

CHAPTER FIFTEEN

TIM LEFT THE HOTEL AND SLUNG THE MUGSHOT BOOK INTO THE BACK of his car. It was unbelievable. He had positive identifications for a Scottish politician, Yuhanaa Islam, Lucky Buchanan, John Hamilton, a rogue that Tim knew had been dead for two years and his own boss, DI Hunter Wilson. He was feeling exasperated when he drew up outside the rehab facility.

He noticed the security cameras follow him as he got out of the car, locked the doors and strode towards the main building. At least they would protect his car, he thought. Then it occurred to him that the cameras would have spotted Lucky too, whenever he left the premises. That might be helpful to the enquiries. Of course, he had known Lucky since their school days. They used to play rugby against each other. Tim knew Lucky was an entitled bully but had never thought of him as inflicting the kind of cruelty that would deprive a victim of their sight. On the other hand, he was an addict. Who knew what an addict could do when they were high?

When he reached the reception desk, Tim rang the bell and a harassed little nurse emerged from a back office.

She looked up at Tim. "My goodness, you're tall."

"I've been told that before."

She blushed to the roots of her ash blonde hair. "Sorry. Now we've got that over with. What can I do for you? Something tells me you're not checking in."

"You're right there, Staff Nurse Jessica." He read the name badge on her chest.

"More's the pity. How can I help?" She smiled, looked directly into his eyes and then continued. "You have amazingly blue eyes." Then she put her hand over her mouth. "I'm so sorry. I can't believe I just said that. How unprofessional of me. I'm exhausted. I've been on shift for sixteen hours. Someone called in sick. I'm babbling now, aren't I?"

"Don't worry, I know what long shifts are like. I'm a police detective." And you are pretty, he thought. "Perhaps if I checked in here, I'd get a bit of peace until my boss tracked me down. What do you think?"

"I'm not sure about that. I know I don't get much peace, that's for sure."

"I can imagine. I don't suppose your patients are permitted to leave the grounds, are they?"

"Oh yes. Especially towards the end of their stay with us. We encourage them to take up a sport, maybe riding or jogging, or even just going for long walks. And if they can go into the village and stop in at the shops or have a cup of tea in one of the wee cafes without coming back high or puggled we can judge that they may be ready for life in the real world."

"I see. And was Lucky Buchanan allowed out in that way?"

"Yes indeed. He's been doing very well."

"Do you keep records of who goes out when?"

"We have to. They sign out, write down what they are going to do in the book and sign back in again."

"I don't suppose I could have a quick look at this book, could I?"

"You could, if you took your arm off it. You're leaning on it." She smiled at Tim as he stepped back and flicked through the few pages to reach the night of Eileen's attack.

"There were two of your patients out that evening," he said.

"Which one? Oh yes, old Archie goes out about that time most nights. He's a keen fisherman and watches the fish coming to the surface of the lake down the road. Apparently, fish don't have any eyelids, so they're more comfortable eating insects in the dark."

"Really? Who knew?" Tim shrugged. "Lucky Buchanan was out as well?"

"He's taken up running and is training for a marathon. He was out for hours. Apparently, he got lost and hurt his foot. He had to hitch-hike back if I recall."

"Hmm. Lucky's taken up running? He's the laziest man I know. Are you sure?"

"You know him? Well, I'm sure." She grinned. "He's even taking a pride in his appearance, grown a beard and everything."

"Wow! Could I get a copy of that page?"

"Aren't you meant to have a warrant or something?"

Tim handed her his card. "I honestly am a detective." He whispered.

She looked left and right and hurried into the back office with the book. She handed him an envelope and replaced the book with care.

"Don't tell anybody."

"I won't."

"Anyway, you still haven't told me why you're here," she said.

"That's easy. I'm here to relieve you of Lord Lachlan Buchanan."

"Lucky? Yes, he's all packed and ready to go and complaining that his chauffeur is late again."

"Chauffeur? I'll give him chauffeur. I'll leave him here if he's not careful."

"Please don't do that. I need the room," she said.

"Timmy boy." Lachlan's voice blasted from the corridor. "I didn't see you arrive. I was looking for your big BMW hybrid thing."

"Morning Lucky. No, I brought the Merc today. It's faster and I want to get you home pronto."

"It may be faster, but it's not so grand, is it?"

"Lucky, do you want me to drive you home, or do you want to get the bus?"

"Don't be like that, Tim. Now don't you go missing me too much Jessie," he said to the nurse. He grabbed her hand and kissed it. "Will you carry my case, Tim? I've hurt my blasted foot."

"No. Now I'm a busy man. Let's go." Tim pointed to his card that Jessie was holding. "If you ever need a punter put in their place, give me a call." He smiled. Then Tim walked past Lucky's suitcase and jumped into the driver's seat.

When they got back to Lucky's estate, he offered Tim a coffee.

"Thanks. I might as well, while we wait for the home security official to arrive. Surely he's not going to tag you around the whole estate. He'd be here all week checking the readings."

"True enough." Lucky rang the bell and asked a young girl who answered to bring coffee for two. "Proper coffee mind, not that instant grit, I've had quite enough of that. And some of Mrs Price's home-made cookies if we have any.

"No, the tag thing is only to kick in at 7.30 pm until 7.30 am. I've to stay within the main part of the house during that time. Of course, the front and back doors and all the French windows are to be taboo, so I can't collect from a dealer. Ridiculous really. If I were desperate, I'd see my dealer at 7.25pm, wouldn't I?"

"I suppose so. Who's your dealer now?"

"Ha ha. You won't trick me that easily Tim. I don't have one now. But rumour has it that, even from prison, Arjun Mansoor has this area pretty well tied up."

Tim watched as the coffee and biscuits were brought in and laid on the coffee table. Lucky dismissed the girl and poured the drinks. He watched Lucky add milk and lots of sugar and reach for two of the biscuits."

"These cookies are delicious." He waved them at Tim. "Try one."

"I will. So, what's with the beard, Lucky?"

"I felt a change come over me in rehab and I wanted that to show it outside as well as inside me. I've always ridden, but I got back to that too at the end of my rehabilitation programme. Can you believe I've also taken up running, going to the gym and doing yoga. There are some nice little coffee places and shops around the village. I even do a bit of cooking. I thought I might enter that TV show *Who wants to be Muster-Chef get that food out of here*, or whatever it's called."

Tim couldn't help laughing. Lucky was an arrogant arse, but he was charming too.

"Aren't those cookies good?"

"Yes they are, Lucky. Very good. You'll need to get the recipe to make them on the show."

The young girl knocked on the door again to announce that there was a Miss Judy McCallum from home security to see Lord Buchanan. She stood back to let the woman in, and Lucky made the introductions.

"You're vouching for Lord Buchanan, are you?" she asked Tim.

"No. I brought him home from rehab and waited with him until you got here. I can confirm that in that time he has had a cup of strong, sweet coffee and two homemade biscuits. Nothing else."

"Won't you be living here?"

"Definitely not," Tim said.

"Who will be with you on the premises, Lord Buchanan?"

Lucky rolled off the names of his few remaining members of staff and their job titles. "My cousin Sir Felix Buchanan will also be staying here when he returns from his present business trip." He added.

"Where is he?"

"Who knows? He went on a trip to do a gig in Ibiza, Tim. He hadn't been there any time at all when I heard he's on his way back. But I can't raise him. He's a damn pest these days. Totally unreliable."

"That's the pot calling the kettle black," Tim said.

The woman explained how the security system worked as she attached the home curfew bracelet to Lucky's ankle and found a convenient power point to plug in the monitor. She explained how it worked again so that there could be no doubt and instructed Lucky to walk to various parts of the house. That enabled her to test the strength of the signal. She stressed the times that his tag would be in operation and then gave him a card with a phone number to call if he had any problems. Then she left as quickly as she had come, telling him she had three more homes to visit before she was finished for the day.

"I have to go too, Lucky, old man."

"Bring my bag in from the car will you, Tim? I've got this bad foot from my running, remember."

"Not a fucking chance. Come and get it yourself, now. Otherwise, I'll take it with me and make a bonfire out of your designer briefs."

"Bastard. Where are you going anyway? Can't you stay and keep me company for a while?"

"No. Don't whine. I have one stop to make on my way home."

When Tim drew up outside Thomson's Top Cars, he looked around the showroom. No sign of Jamie. He wasn't surprised.

Frankie was on the phone in the office and Tim waved to him and walked towards the help desk where Donna was sitting flicking through a wedding magazine.

"DC Myerscough, what can I do for you?" Donna said.

"I really wanted to see how Jamie and Linda are. I should have worked out they wouldn't be here."

"Linda never is, but anyways, she and Jamie are at the hospital waiting for them to wake up her sister. They say it should happen today."

Frankie finished his call and walked towards them. "It's

right bloody awful. Some bastard took her eyes. Did you know that? How does anyone even do that? What's going to happen to her? I don't know." Frankie shook his head.

"God alone knows. But we'll do our best to catch him."

"Make it sooner, will you? If Jamie gets to him first, I'll need to find another best man for my wedding. He'll be doing life."

"We'll do our best. But on a happier note, you two are planning your wedding, already I see." Tim nodded towards Donna's magazine. "Set a date yet?"

"Nah. Not till Uncle Ian's out. How's yer pop?"

"Still driving me mad."

"Much like Uncle Ian, then." Frankie grinned.

I can't help being a bit worried that this one lived. There seems to be a connection between her family and the police. It would have been so much easier if she'd died like the others. Because she was young and pretty, there is too much sympathy for her. I don't like it.

It's not just that, but the newspapers are full of identikit photos of me, but luckily not one of them bears any resemblance to me. Maybe I should shave my beard off, or would that be too obvious?

Anyway, I've got a great alibi and I can't be two places at once. Nobody can, can they?

CHAPTER
SIXTEEN

"How on earth can you park in such tight spaces, Nadia? I'd need at least an extra couple of yards."

"It comes from doing deliveries for my uncle's restaurant, otherwise I'd end up walking miles every shift."

"I am benefitting from your laziness, then."

"Cheers Colin. Kindly said."

"Kindly meant. Shall we go in and see if we can find the manager? The hotel's own CCTV should provide us with some answers."

"I hope so. Let's go."

They walked up the steps into the foyer of the hotel and gazed at their surroundings in silence. It was almost as bright inside as outside because the light from the chandelier bounced off the shining surfaces.

"I wouldn't like to be in charge of the dusting here," Nadia said.

"I wouldn't want to have to change those lightbulbs." Colin whispered.

"May I help you?" A supercilious voice crossed the space towards them.

They walked towards the voice and found the owner to be a tall man of late middle age who worked behind the reception counter. Colin pulled out his identity card and the man examined it as if it were a priceless gem before returning it with a sneer.

"How may I be of assistance, Detective Sergeant Reid? And you are?" He asked Nadia.

Nadia handed him her card too. "DC Nadia Chan. We wondered if we might have a word with the manager, please."

"He is rather busy right now; may I be of service?"

"We're here about the attempted murder that occurred here on Saturday. I think that takes priority over whatever he has going on," Colin said. He spoke deliberately loudly.

"Murder?" asked an elderly lady who was standing next to him. "Ooh how exciting. I do like those murder mystery parties. Is that it?"

"The gentleman will have his little joke, Mrs Haverstock." The man attempted to laugh.

"The last time I thought about it, murder was no laughing matter," Colin said.

"Of course, not, Sir. Not just now Mrs Haverstock, but shall I put it in the suggestion box?" The man asked. Then he turned back to Colin. "Please keep your voice down. Will you, DS Reid?"

"May we speak to the manager now?"

Colin and Nadia watched while the man picked up the phone and dialled. He turned his back and whispered into the mouthpiece.

"The manager will be with you shortly. Now I must help Mrs Haverstock. May I assist you further dear lady?"

They watched while the woman glowed under the attention of the hotelier.

"Some people are easily pleased," Nadia said.

"True, but they are not usually the patrons of The Waldorf Astoria. I am the manager here, Vikram Mandal, I understand you require my assistance. Follow me and we'll talk in my office. Will you take tea?"

"No, no tea thank you, Mr Mandal," Colin said.

The office was small, but well-appointed and contained a large desk and more power points than Nadia thought possible, never mind necessary.

Colin explained to the manager that his staff had assisted them by providing their recollections of what the attacker looked like and asked if they might study the CCTV of the relevant day.

"Indeed, this person must be apprehended as a priority. Come this way. I'm afraid the room that houses the CCTV is rather small, but we do keep our film for at least thirty days. Which areas of the hotel do you want to see?"

"Probably just the foyer, the bar and the restaurant. Unless there is CCTV in the lifts."

"Sadly not. That is an improvement planned for next year. It may be advanced, now, of course." The manager's expression was solemn. "This attack is an appalling slight on our brand. Nothing like it has ever happened to one of our guests, not anywhere in the world. The publicity is most unwelcome. Please let me know if there is anything I or any member of my staff can do to bring the perpetrator to justice."

"I'll be sure to tell the victim you're thinking of her, Mr Mandal," Nadia said.

"Be assured that we are. We have sent flowers. They are cheerful. Very colourful."

"She's blind, Mr Mandal. She can't see the colours. Now could you send in a member of staff to show us how your system works? Then just leave us to do our job."

"Colin, this is hopeless. So far, I haven't found a single person matching the general description coming into the foyer. I hope you're having better luck in the bar."

"Well, I've found the boss. He's sitting waiting for Meera and there's a bottle of champagne on ice next to his table."

"That'll cost a pretty penny in here. I wonder what they're celebrating. Meera keeps looking at her left hand."

"Ooh, now I wonder if he finally proposed. That would be a fun fact, but we better keep that little piece of deduction under our hats."

"I'm not wearing one. Wait, Colin, this could be our man. Tall, dark hair and I can't tell if that's a beard or a shadow because of his large hat. Who wears hats like that nowadays?"

"A man avoiding detection, perhaps. Slow it down."

"It is slowed down. I still can't see him properly," Nadia said.

"What about that woman. She's covered from head to toe, but look at her shoes, they're not at all feminine and they're huge."

"Give it up with the big feet. My niece wears a size nine."

"A nine? Goodness, and here's you with your dainty size threes."

"You'll get my size three up your arse, if you're not careful. Then tell me how dainty it feels."

"Funny girl. How about that guy? I know he's limping, but he's definitely got dark hair and a beard."

"Yeh, he seems tall too. I just can't see his face because, he's got his head down all the time. It's almost as if he knows where the cameras are."

"Look, there's our victim joining him in the bar. Let's see if any of the staff can identify him from the CCTV shot and our mugshot book."

"I thought Tim was doing mugshots?"

"Yes, but he didn't have the CCTV," Colin said.

The newly seconded DC Larkin was thrilled to have a task of his own. He called HMP Edinburgh and found that Arjun Mansoor was still incarcerated, but he did get out on day release as he was nearing the end of his sentence. He had been out on the day in question, but the times didn't match up with when the attacker met Eileen for dinner.

He had better luck with Lord Lachlan Buchanan. He was still enrolled in his rehab centre, but had been out, with permission, late into the evening. The nurse Neil spoke to said Lord Buchanan was training for a marathon and preferred to run in the evening when it was cooler.

Neil then called Lord Buchanan himself. He wanted to establish if his story would match that of the nurse. He was confused when Lucky said little about that except to confirm that was also his recollection, then went off on a rant about his cousin, Sir Felix Buchanan.

Lucky explained that Felix was meant to be living with

him, but he didn't know where he was. Felix had a habit of going off and doing his own thing, it wasn't unusual. Lucky emphasised that he had no idea where the bounder was, and that was why he had asked his friend DC Tim Myerscough to sign him out of rehab and bring him home.

What a lot of nonsense he had to listen to in this job, however, Neil thanked him and made a note to check that story with Tim later.

The last person on Neil's list was a former DC, John Hamilton. Neil knew this guy had a reputation for being prickly, so he would have to tread carefully. He called the number he had been given for John but was disappointed when a woman's voice told him that John had moved.

"Gone down to North Berwick, I think cos he's working with his brother down there. Estate Agents they are. Sorry, I can't be more help."

Neil thanked the woman and stared at his notebook. Then he began to look up Estate Agents in North Berwick from the list Google brought up on his phone.

There is no doubt that eyes are fascinating. Did you know that the way the eyes work mean that we see everything upside down? They think babies see upside down and can't see things the right way up for the first few days of life until their brains work out that they need to flip the images they're getting to make sense of them. Personally, I doubt babies can focus on anything very much, except their mother's nipples. I can understand that.

In fact, any image focussed by the eye on the retina is always inverted, so we see things upside down and back to front. It is said that eyes are the mirrors of the soul, but they are just mechanical parts of the body. Transferring the images from inverted pictures to information each person can use is simply due to the way the eye and its lens system works. The front of the eye is curved. That means it bends light and this creates the upended image on the retina. The retina is a complex part of the eye. Its purpose is to turn light into signals and pictures that the brain understands and can use to navigate the world.

On top of all that there is a beautiful array of colours of eyes. Some of the colours are rare. Those are ones that need to be added to the collection.

CHAPTER SEVENTEEN

"Right," Hunted banged the desk in front of him with a folder. "A little quiet, please." He pointed to the white board. "Eileen Maguire, what did she have to say for herself, Rachael?"

"She has been woken from her coma and knows that she has lost her eyes. She's been told that she'll never see again."

"That will take some time to process."

"Yes boss. She told Mel and me that she met her date online. I said it might not have been him who attacked her, but she dismissed that as incredible, and I'm inclined to agree with her."

"So do I. Meera and I must have come across her shortly after the deed was done and there was no sign of the date then. He must have attacked her and scarpered."

"Miserable rotten coward," Neil said.

Rachael nodded and then went on, "She gave us two descriptions of the man. In the photos on the dating site, he was pictured at an angle that made his legs seem long. He appeared to be muscular, and Eileen used the word sexy. He was pictured on the beach at North Berwick with the Bass Rock behind him and he had a dog. She thought it was a golden Labrador."

"She'll be needing her own dog, soon," Nadia said.

"Long waiting list for a guide dog." Colin commented. He picked up the half-eaten apple that lay on the desk beside him and took another bite.

"Maybe not too long." Tim whispered in Colin's ear.

"We're getting side-tracked. I make it a rule not to get side-tracked. What was the other description, Rachael?"

"Well, she said when they spoke on the phone, she could always only see his face. He had dark hair and a dark bushy beard, but there was no red in the beard."

"What do you mean?"

"Well, I'm no expert, boss, but most men I know who have dark hair have some red colour through their beards and I wondered if it might be a fake if it was uniform dark-haired colour."

"Could be, interesting thought."

"Anyway, when they met in the bar, the lighting was low, probably on purpose to make it seem romantic."

"Yes, it was. Meera commented on it."

"But when the date, Frederick he called himself, got up to greet her, Eileen remembered thinking that he wasn't as tall as she had expected, and he had a slight limp."

"We spotted a dark-haired man with a beard on the CCTV who had a limp. But we couldn't get a good look at his face. We took a screen shot anyway," Colin said.

"Tim, who did our ever-vigilant witnesses identify from the mugshots you showed them?" Hunter asked.

"Yuhanaa Islam."

"The MSP?"

"Yes, the MSP I was playing squash with that evening."

"Okay, who else?"

"Sir Felix Buchanan."

"Isn't he that bloody awful cousin of Lucky's who was a few years below us at school?" Bear asked.

"Yes, but he was at Fettes."

"I know, thank God we didn't have to put up with him at Merchiston Castle."

"We had enough idiots of our own, if you remember, Bear."

"Lovely as it is to reminisce, young Myerscough, could you and Bear bring yourselves back to the present long enough for you to complete the list of suspects?"

"Why is Sir Felix amongst your mugshots? I don't remember the name," Hunter said.

"Sorry, boss. I put him in to see if people could distinguish between him and Lucky. They look quite similar."

"And could they?"

"Apparently not. However, Arjun Mansoor and John Hamilton, were identified, also that old a rogue who died in the pile up on the A68 a couple of years ago, and, of course, your good self, boss."

"Well at least the boss was there. Yuhanaa Islam and the dead guy were definitely not, yet there they are on the list," Mel said.

"I called the jail about Mansoor. He does get out for day release, but has to be back by 5.30, so he was behind bars when the attack took place," Neil said.

"Yes, but he's a wily one. I wouldn't bet against him orchestrating something like that," Hunter said.

"But why? Did he even know Eileen?"

"No, but his arch enemy's son dates her sister," Tim said.

"Would he even know that? Why not go after Jamie or even Linda rather than Eileen? I mean it's all a bit one-step removed, isn't it?" Hunter mused.

"When I phoned the number I had for John Hamilton, I was told he's moved to North Berwick. He's working as an estate agent with his brother," Neil said.

"Frederick told Eileen that he lived in North Berwick," Mel said.

"He did, but can we put any credence on anything he told the poor girl?" Hunter looked sad as he thought about Eileen. He wasn't sure he'd ever get over the sight of her on the lift floor. He had seen many horrible things in his life, but her raw eye sockets had to be one of the worst. "Anyway, we'll have to find out which estate agents he's with."

"I've done a phone round, boss. I tracked him down to the one on the High Street, National and Local Homes. Two estate agents named Hamilton work there, Hector and John."

"Well done, Neil."

"Might I be the one to interview John, boss?"

"Probably not, Colin. He was your partner for too long. It'll probably be anybody but you. What about this Felix man? Where was he on the night in question?"

"No idea, boss. He's Lucky's cousin and apparently, he's gone AWOL. At least, that's what Lucky said and why he needed me to meet him from rehab and take him home. Someone reputable had to be there when they officer came to put his tag on."

"Someone reputable? I suppose he couldn't find anybody,

and that's why he asked you," Bear said. "What with that and the boss being identified as a suspect in our case, we've got our work cut out for us this time."

CHAPTER EIGHTEEN

Jamie sat sulking on the sofa. His beer was getting warm, and Linda wouldn't speak to him. He was damned if he was going to crack first and order the pizza for tea.

"Come on Linda, you know I've got to do something. We need that place to go up for sale faster than ever now that Eileen's going to stay with us."

"Eileen will be in rehab for ages, Jamie Thomson. Don't you use my sister as an excuse for the nonsense schemes you and your pop came up with."

"It was just a stupid mouse. Did you hear old Mrs Morrison squeal? It was well funny."

"No it wasn't. The poor soul."

"Believe me, anybody who hangs around with Arjun Mansoor is not a poor soul. Look, enough of this. Frankie and Donna will be home with the twins soon and it's our turn to get tea ready. Are you going to phone for pizza, or am I?"

"Hah! I knew you would give in eventually. Let's get a pepperoni and a veggie supreme."

"Both with stuffed crusts, right?"

"If you insist." Linda smiled.

Frankie and Donna arrived with the girls at the same time as the pizza delivery guy jumped off his bike.

"Ooh girls, look at that, Uncle Jamie has got pizza for tea," Frankie said.

"Pizza." The girls giggled and rubbed their tummies in unison.

Their reverie was broken moments later when Mrs Morrison next door screamed loudly and shouted for her husband. The twins burst into tears.

"What a fright I got," Donna said.

"So did the girls, look at them. You take them in, and I'll go to see if the neighbours need any help." Frankie jumped over the little garden fence and asked Mrs Morrison if there was anything he could do.

"Yes. You can lock up that maniac cousin of yours and throw away the key. I'm sick of him. Can't wait till we move."

"What's happened? What's Jamie done this time?"

"This morning it was a mouse in my porch and now look." The woman stood to one side and there was one dead cat lying across her doorstep. "He's mad. A danger to humanity. Needs locking up."

"Jamie may be a pain, Mrs Morrison, but I honestly don't think he'd hurt an animal."

"Hurt? Hurt? That cat's dead. Any fool can see that. If you want to help, throw away the cat and then get rid of your obnoxious cousin. I'm phoning the police. I won't put up with any more of this. Arjun warned us about you lot, but this is worse than I could ever imagine."

. . .

About an hour later, pizza devoured and Jamie and Linda back on speaking terms, Frankie and Donna took the girls up for their bath and story before bedtime. It was then the doorbell rang.

Jamie opened the door to Mel and Bear. "You know she's only with you until me and Linda split, don't you, big man."

"Mel has told me that you think you're irresistible, Jamie. But this isn't a social call. We've had a complaint from your neighbours."

"That'll be the Morrisons next door. You better come in."

Jamie led them into the living room and waited while Linda muted the TV.

"What's the old bat saying now?" he asked.

"Your neighbours claim that you placed a live mouse into their porch yesterday and that it gave Mrs Morrison a terrible fright," Mel said.

"Aw, poor soul got a fright. Well, yes, I did put the mouse in there, but, before you ask, that deed cat was nowt to do with me. No' my style at all. You know me, Mel. I'm a lover not a fighter."

"To be honest, I didn't think it would be you. But just keep your distance, Jamie and give the Morrisons a wide berth. Will you?"

"I can't promise that Mel. Sorry. They live right next door. Unless they want to move, that is."

"Take this as a formal warning, Jamie. No more nonsense at the Morrisons'," Bear said.

Jamie looked at him. "More to the point, have you found the scumbag that attacked Eileen? That's more important than a fright with a mouse or a dead cat on the doorstep. That was proper grim."

"Yes it was. That's why I don't have time to come chasing you about playing pranks on your neighbours."

"No pranks, Mel, this is business. Now what about it?"

"You know I can't tell you much, but we do have various suspects and lines of enquiry. Our colleague DC Rachael Anderson has been appointed Eileen's VSO."

"What does that mean, VSO?" Linda asked.

"Sorry Linda, Victim Support Officer. Rachael will keep Eileen up to date with our enquiries."

"Eileen will be going into rehab when she leaves hospital. Will you tell your colleague?"

"No problem." Bear smiled.

"But you may never find him,"

"We have to," Mel said. "This man has not only attacked you sister, but we believe he was involved in two murders as well. We will catch this monster and put him away for good."

CHAPTER NINETEEN

Neil slowed down and Nadia checked the numbers on the doors. When they found the right estate agents there was nowhere convenient to park, so they spent the next five minutes touring the side streets of North Berwick looking for a likely space.

"Stop Neil. There's one."

"It's too small. I'll never get in there."

"Then shift, because I will."

She wriggled over to the driver's seat so fast that Neil hardly had time to get out of the car. He tried to help by guiding her in, but his actions were superfluous.

"I had heard rumours about your parking skills, but that was amazing."

"It was a bit of a tight squeeze, but I did it."

"How do we get out again?"

"That's your problem, you wanted to drive. Now let's go and have a chat with the Hamiltons."

Nadia showed her id to the young woman behind the reception desk and asked if they could speak to John and

Hector Hamilton. The girl informed them that Hector was out seeing a client, but that John was in.

She lifted the phone and rang through to John. Nadia noticed that it took the man a long time to get from his office behind a wall to greet them. Maybe he's emptying his bowels, she thought uncharitably.

As John led them through to his office, Nadia noted the man had put on even more weight since the last time she had seen him. She wondered if he'd given up the drugs and his appetite had increased. She and Neil took the seats opposite John, and she introduced them both and showed him their id.

"Colin not coming to see me then? That's a relief. He always was a boring old stickler for the rules."

"Yes, he still is," Neil said.

Nadia led the questioning and Neil made notes of the replies.

She noticed that the room was cool, but John was sweating.

"Are you ill?" she asked.

"No, why?"

"You seem to be sweating and it's not hot in here. I wondered if you were ill, or abusing drugs again. If you're not sick, it must be the latter."

"Ha-ha, very funny. I just get nervous when the police roll into my office and try to frame me."

"I'll not frame you. It wouldn't be a pretty picture. Relax, Mr Hamilton," Nadia then began to ask John about where he was living now.

John confirmed that he had moved from Tranent to North Berwick as a vacancy had come up in the company his brother worked for, and he had put John forward for an interview. He was living with his brother in his flat in a converted Georgian villa. Property prices were much higher in North Berwick than Tranent, but he hoped to get his own place sooner rather than later.

He showed them a picture of his brother. Like John he had dark hair, but Hector also sported a big black bushy beard.

"Where was the photo taken?" Neil asked. "That looks like a grand building in the background."

"It's just outside my brother's place. It must have been a fine house before the developers got hold of it and sub-divided it into flats. We live in this part here." John pointed to the first floor and drew a circle with his finger around two windows. "There are six two bedroomed flats in what was once a home for one family. Amazing thought, isn't it?"

Nadia wanted to move their questions on from property. That was not the point of their visit today. In answer to her questions, John confirmed that he did use dating websites, but he had never used the one that Eileen enrolled with, and he had never heard of Eileen Maguire.

"Anyway," he said, "I'm going out with Katy now."

"Who's Katy?" Nadia asked.

"The woman we spoke to when you arrived. She's a bit young for you, isn't she?" Neil asked.

"Since when was that a matter for a police enquiry? But no, that's Gemma our new receptionist. Katy's an agent like me and she's out showing a house right now."

Neil shrugged and Nadia started asking more questions.

John stated that he had not been in Edinburgh on the date of the attack. He remembered this because his brother had been out, and he and Katy had had the flat to themselves. It had been a wild night of passion.

Nadia swallowed hard. She then asked John if he had ever dined at the Pompadour Restaurant at the Waldorf Astoria.

His bitter laughter was loud and long. "Darling, I have never even had a glass of water in The Caledonian Hotel as it was. And believe me, contrary to popular opinion, the commissions in this game are not so great that I anticipate changing the habits of a lifetime soon."

Nadia snapped that she was not his darling and that she and DC Larkin would require to follow up this interview by speaking to John's brother and girlfriend. She handed him her card and marched out of the room and back to the car without a backward glance.

She completely forgot she had planned to have some amusement watching Neil extract the car from the parking space and jumped into the driver's seat. She noticed that Neil had just got his seatbelt fastened before she extricated the vehicle and drove in silence back to the station.

CHAPTER TWENTY

Tim knocked on Hunter's door. "Got a minute boss?"

"Always got time for a hard-working member of the team, and even for you, young Myerscough. Help yourself to a decent coffee."

"That's the real reason I came in."

"I know but sing for your supper by telling me about Lord Lachlan Buchanan, why don't you. I have a darts match at The Persevere Bar tonight and I could do with some good news before I go."

Tim poured himself a full mug of the excellent coffee that Hunter kept brewing in his room. The smell permeated the whole floor, but few were invited to partake of the nectar.

"Thanks boss." He held up his mug. "I picked up Lucky from rehab yesterday, and there was a pretty little nurse at reception. We got on well."

"Cut the romancing and get to the main course."

Tim smiled. "She explained to me that, as the patients get towards the end of their rehabilitation, they are encouraged to go out into the village. The CCTV on the grounds is extensive, but other than that they are not watched. There are a few shops in the village and a couple of little cafes where they can begin to mix in the outside world."

"Hmm. Do we know where Lord Buchanan was on the evening Eileen was attacked?"

"Each patient who leaves the grounds has to sign out, say where they're going and sign back in again."

"Okay."

"Jessie, that's the nurse, told me that Lucky has taken up riding again but also taken up running. He is training for a marathon."

"Is this the same Lord Buchanan?"

"That's what I thought, but apparently so. Jessie told me Lucky prefers to run after dinner when the temperature drops, so he was out training the evening Eileen was attacked."

"But we only have his word for that."

"That's what he wrote in the book."

"Not good enough, Tim. Arrange for a uniform to pick him up and we'll question him here."

"He's on the tag. He'll have to be home by seven thirty."

"He won't be late. I thought he had that parasite cousin of his living with him too. Why were you roped into picking up Lucky?"

"Felix is away. He fancies himself as an internationally renowned DJ and does gigs in Europe when he can."

"Does he now? Get Lord Buchanan in here."

Hunter wandered through to the incident room. "You busy, Bear?"

"Always, boss. How can I help?"

"Arjun Mansoor was one of the faces identified by our witnesses, I want you and Neil to take a run over to Saughton and have a chat with him. And make sure with the prison officers that there's no way he could have been outside the walls, check his visitors. You know the drill."

"Can I have a word with you, boss?" Rachael asked.

"Is everything okay with Eileen?"

"Yes, it's not that, but there's something I need to ask you."

"That sounds ominous. Am I going to like it?"

"Possibly not."

I didn't think so. You better come through to my office, Rachael, and tell me all about it.

"That's interesting, one of Mansoor's visitors was Mr Morrison," Bear said.

"Who the hell is Mr Morrison?"

"He and his wife live next door to Frankie Hope and Jamie Thomson. And it's Jamie's bidie-ins sister who got attacked."

"Hello big man. What brings you to this illustrious residence?"

Bear recognised the voice. "Hi Jamie."

"We've just been interviewing Arjun Mansoor and checking his whereabouts the day of the attack," Neil said.

Bear frowned at him, but he wasn't looking.

"He was here you numpties, all locked up nice and tight. But did I hear you saying Mr Morrison was in visiting? Is Arjun behind that attack? I'll fucking see him hang, if he is."

"Calm down Jamie. You're right. Arjun was here. No chance he did it. We just had to check because he was identified by a witness, wrongly as it happens."

"Aye but he could of been behind it big man, we both know he's got a long reach. But so have I and my pop's longer."

"Don't do anything foolish Jamie. Are you here to visit your pop?" Bear asked.

"Aye, I am that. I have a feeling Arjun might trip on his way back from Chapel on Sunday. Shame that."

There are too many police on the prowl about Eileen's attack. I don't like it. I just wish it would all calm down and I could get on with my life. She'll want to get on with her life too. Or I suppose she will. I wonder if she ever wishes she'd died like the others. Or maybe she's happy just to be alive. I suppose it depends how you look at things.

I don't think there's any chance of them identifying me. I hope not.

CHAPTER TWENTY-ONE

HUNTER OPENED THE DOOR FOR MEERA AS THEY STEPPED INTO HIS local pub, The Persevere Bar, for a drink. He noticed the captain of his darts team at the bar.

"Hello Clouseau, fancy throwing a few arrows before the match?"

"No thanks, Jim. Meera and I are just in for a quick drink before it starts."

"Then, don't tell me, you and your lovely lady will go upstairs without me."

"That's guaranteed. What's not is whether there's anything in the fridge that'll make a meal."

"Nice to see you, Meera," Jim said. "Tom's due in shortly. We'll get the match started then."

Hunter ordered a red wine for Meera, pints for himself and Jim and took a seat with Meera at the far corner of the pub.

"Any word from Ailsa on that poor girl?"

"Shocking, isn't it? Ailsa said she's never seen anything like it." Meera sipped her drink and went on. "Apparently her name is Eileen Maguire, and her sister is Linda. Could that be Jamie Thomson's girlfriend?"

"It is. Tim took them up to the hospital. From the autopsy, does it seem the first two attacks were carried out by the same person?"

"Yes, thank goodness. We wouldn't want more than one nutter like that running around."

"I agree. Still, although Eileen's injuries are horrendous, she did see the man and can describe him to us."

"Surely the staff at the hotel can do that too."

"Yes, they've done that. One of the suspects appears to be me."

"I'll vouch for you, darling," Meera said. She sat in silence, drinking her wine and thinking about the future Eileen faced. It was only when Hunter touched her arm that her thoughts came back into the room.

"Shall we have another before my match?"

"Yes, Hunter, let's do that."

"I'm thrilled that we won that match. I didn't think we had a hope, but I'm sorry it was just bacon and eggs for dinner," Hunter said.

"And tomato. Don't forget the tomato. Why do you always have your heating go off so early? It's freezing in here."

"Just so I can watch your nipples becoming erect before I suck them."

"You are a bad boy, Hunter Wilson."

"But don't tell anybody, it'll ruin my image." He cuddled up beside her in bed. "Gosh you are cold," he said.

"I told you. It's freezing. Feel my feet." She raised her foot to warm it on his groin."

"Oh Meera, you bitch." He gasped. "Let's warm you up, woman."

They began their foreplay slowly and gently, right up until the time Hunter's phone rang.

"You better tell me you're going to ignore that," Meera said.

"Yep." He rolled on top of her and felt her legs spread underneath him inviting him in.

The phone rang again.

"Don't you dare. Hunter, don't you dare."

He slid inside her and they continued caressing each other long after they had come.

"You are beautiful," he said. "Why is a brilliant, beautiful woman like you going out with a lowly DI?"

"I keep asking myself the very same thing."

"Now who's the bad one?" he asked. His phone rang again. "Is madam sufficiently satisfied that I may now look at my phone and find out who's trying to get hold of me?"

"She is, indeed."

"Thank God for that. I'm spent." He rolled over and picked up his phone. "Bugger, it's Tim and I've got five missed calls. I better phone back."

"Thanks for calling back, boss. You remember that Lucky asked me to pick him up from rehab because his cousin had gone walk about?"

"Did you call me at this time of night to remind me of that?"

"No boss."

"Then cut to the chase, young Myerscough."

"Felix has re-appeared at Lucky's estate. He's saying he

went to Ibiza, but Lucky says that he seems anxious because he thinks Felix said that the Spanish police have issued a warrant for his arrest."

"Then why didn't they stop him at the border? What's he been up to?"

"Lucky said that Felix thinks it's for assault. He wants me to sort it out because he says it's a misunderstanding and Felix is innocent."

"Of course, he does. I take it Felix isn't going anywhere tonight."

"Doubt it, boss."

"Then we'll have a briefing tomorrow at eight. See if you can find out anymore by then."

"Yes boss."

"And Tim, next time, make sure it's urgent."

CHAPTER TWENTY-TWO

Hunter looked around the room and did a quick head count. They were all there. Good he wouldn't have to introduce this new guy more than once. He took a sip of his coffee and whispered to the man just to double check how to pronounce his name. His was a good team that he could depend on, he hoped the new detective would fit in well. Then he called the room to order.

"Bear do you and Tim have breakfast here just to irritate me, or is there another reason that I'm not aware of?"

"There are several reasons, boss. Irritating you is an added bonus." The big man grinned. "Anyway, why pick on us? Colin's eating too. That apple doesn't stand a chance in the hands of a detective sergeant."

"Funny man," Hunter said. "Right, pay attention, we have a new member of the team this morning. DI Oskar Krol has joined us from Dunfermline, Fife."

"Are you sure he's not from Gdansk, Poland, boss?" Colin asked.

"Good guess, but no, originally from Krakow, now living in

Dunfermline with my wife Heather and kids Luke and Daisy. Any more questions?" the man spoke in flawless but slightly accentuated English. He looked around the room and met the gaze of each person there.

"So boss, are you still pretending to be DCI Mackay and DI Krol is now pretending to be you?"

"Nobody is pretending to be anybody, Bear. I am acting DCI and DI Krol is our new DI. He is a permanent member of our team, so do your best to make a good impression, all of you."

"We'll do our best, boss, but that may not last long," Tim said.

"Right, while the illusion is being sustained, what did you find out about Eileen, yesterday, Rache?"

"She's still adjusting to her new normal and she'll have to have some months of rehab before she goes home."

"How is she reacting to that?"

"I don't it's really sunk in properly because she's not reacting much. Jamie and Linda want her to move in with them, at least for a while when she gets out, but the house is really crowded already. We'll see."

"I wouldn't fancy having to live with Jamie Thomson at the best of times, but especially not being able to see what he's up to. And it's weird. Eileen still has her tear ducts, so she still cries tears, but her eyes are gone. Of course you can't see the sockets, she's still bandaged up, but you can see wet tears running down her cheeks," Mel said.

"What did she tell you about her date?"

"Not much new. She said they met online and the first photos she saw of him showed a tall man with long legs and a beard. He was pictured with a dog on the beach at North

Berwick. She also said his accent was local and that she'd recognise his voice. But I wasn't able to get much more from her so Mel and I will need to go back when Eileen is more able to cope with questions. She seems keen to help all she can to catch this man."

"Mel, when I spoke to John Hamilton. He has moved to North Berwick to work as an estate agent with his brother. He's moved in with his brother too," Nadia said. "His brother was out with clients as was his girlfriend, but I told him we'd need to speak with both of them."

"Interesting. Where do they live?" Hunter asked.

"In a flat, converted from a large house on the outskirts of North Berwick. Apparently, there are six flats in the property now. They live on the middle floor."

"Eileen's date said he lived in a large house on the edge of the town, with his cousin," Rachael said.

"Although Eileen's date may not live anywhere near North Berwick. How much of what he told her can we believe?" Hunter asked.

"Just like John Hamilton may not have a girlfriend," Colin said.

"Eileen did say that her date, Frederick was the name he used, wasn't as tall as she thought he would be when she met him compared to how he looked in the photos on the dating website. But he had the same dark hair and brown eyes and a dark beard," Rachael said. "I asked her if there was any red colour in his beard and she said no, it was just dark. To be honest, boss we couldn't question her for very long, the nurses wouldn't allow it."

"Can we get copies of the photos from the dating company?"

"They won't release them. Data protection or something."

"How about client protection so that they don't get their eyes hacked out of their faces?" Hunter smacked the desk angrily.

"John isn't all that tall," Tim said quietly.

"Nobody's that tall compared to you," Mel said. "We did see Jamie Thomson and Linda when we were coming out from Eileen, and they were going in. Jamie is keen to learn the identity of Eileen's attacker and give them rough justice."

"That's all I bloody need," Hunter said. "What did you find out, Tim?"

"Each member of staff seemed to identify a different mugshot, boss, including you."

"Admittedly I was there. Who else do we have in the frame?"

"Lucky, Felix, John and Arjun Mansoor."

"Boss, remember when I spoke to the duty officer at HMP Edinburgh," Neil said.

"He told me that Mansoor does get out on day release as he's nearing the end of his sentence, but I made sure the times don't match up with the attack. Our guy was out in the evening, for a meal. Mansoor has to be back at Saughton by 5.30. I don't think they let him back out again for dinner dates, but admittedly I didn't ask."

Hunter noticed that Neil was pleased to have information to add to the briefing.

"I agree that's a safe bet," Hunter said.

"I was told the same when I went to the prison," Bear said.

"Good. And Tim have you managed to find out any more about that Spanish arrest warrant against Felix Buchanan?"

"I'm waiting on a call back, boss. I know Felix is back at the estate with Lucky."

"How long was he away? It can't have been long."

"A few days, no more than that. He wasn't making much sense when he called me last night."

"No change there then," Bear said.

"Chase that up, Tim and let me know what the Spanish say. In the meantime," Hunter said. Then he paused as he thought for a moment. Then he looked up. "Rachael, you and Mel go back to see what more you can get from Eileen now. She might have remembered something or be able to speak to you in more detail. Did you and Nadia get anything from the CCTV in the hotel, Colin?"

"I think we've got a likely suspect. He always keeps his head down. Seems to know where the hotel cameras are."

"See if the computer boffins can enhance any of the photo frames, will you?"

"Of course, boss."

"Oskar, I'm not happy about the coincidences between what Eileen said and the changes in John Hamilton's life. I don't believe in coincidences," Hunter said to his new DI.

"That's something we have in common. Do you want me to organise a warrant?"

"Do you think we have enough?"

"I can try. Office and flat?"

"Definitely."

CHAPTER
TWENTY-THREE

It's amazing to think that the colour of your eyes is dictated by the amount of melanin in your body. I find it so interesting. Melanin is a type of pigment, and it gives the specific colour to a person's hair, skin and, most importantly for the collection, the eyes of each of us. The appearance of the iris, that's the coloured ring around the eye's black pupil, depends on how much of the natural pigment it contains. The more melanin in your iris, the darker your eyes will look. Of course, none of us can choose our melanin levels; they are determined by the genes we inherit from our ancestors.

For example, my irises are dark brown, so my eyes have more melanin than light coloured eyes. Elizabeth Taylor's eyes had an extremely specific, and rare, amount of melanin, as a result of which her eyes were a rare violet colour. Of course, there are various shades of light eyes: blues, greens and greys, with many in-between. Violet may have been Taylor's pigmentation, she had pale skin too. That would also be affected by the amount of melanin she had. I had never seen truly violet eyes until I saw Eileen's. They were stunning. I had to add them to the collection. You can understand, can't you?

It is just a bit inconvenient that she survived. I must be careful she can't be aware that I'm around, watching how she's managing.

Mel and Rachael arrived back at the hospital. With parking at a premium, Mel decided that she would chance her luck and stick a 'Police on Call' note in the windscreen, rather than faffing about trying find a space. She looked at Rachael and shrugged and then the detectives made their way towards the reception. Mel asked if Eileen was still in ICU and was pleased to learn that she had been well enough to be moved to a high dependency bed. She thought of that as progress, bearing in mind the long road to recovery ahead of Eileen.

Mel followed Rachael along the corridor to the lift and just as the door was closing a man stuck his arm in to stop the motion. The doors opened and Rachael held the button to allow him time to enter. He smiled, thanked them and then turned away from them to face the door. He pressed the same number of floor that the detectives were going to. It's a busy hospital, Mel thought.

She stood staring idly at the back of the man's head. He stood just under six foot tall and his thick, dark hair was neatly trimmed. She couldn't see his face but had noticed that he had a bushy, moustache and heavy dark stubble. It would be easy to add a costume beard to his chin and make him into their attacker.

Now she was being silly, she thought.

They all got out of the lift on the same floor and turned to walk in the same direction towards the high dependency wards. Coincidence thought Mel.

"The boss doesn't like coincidences," she said.

"What? No, he doesn't." Rachael agreed. "What made you say that?"

"I'll tell you later. Hang back a bit."

Mel slowed her pace and Rachael followed suit. It allowed Mel to watch the man speak to the nurse behind the desk. Then he turned and caught sight of the detectives walking slowly towards him. He turned to walk away and passed them as he went back towards the lift.

"Who was that man?" Mel asked the nurse.

"Mr Donovan? He came to see Miss Maguire."

"And who is Mr Donovan when he's at home?"

"He's her lawyer, not that it's any of your business. Now, how can I help you?"

"Mel showed the nurse her id. We are here to see Miss Maguire too. And believe me, when we're investigating two murders and a brutal attack, everything is our business. Why did he leave in such a hurry without seeing her?"

"He said he'd forgotten his briefcase. He's gone to get it. He said he'll be back soon."

"I'm going to speak to the staff nurse to see if you're allowed to go in to see Miss Maguire. Wait here."

The senior nurse that Mel and Rachael had seen the previous day came towards them. She was smiling. Detectives Anderson and Grant, isn't it?"

Mel nodded. "That's us. We wondered if we could have a bit more of a chat with Eileen Maguire today."

"I don't see a problem with that. She's much better, but to be honest, I don't think the enormity of her injury has really hit her yet. She's in the room second on the left, but please don't tire her out too much. But I do think it will be good for her to think she is being helpful."

"We'll do our best." Mel led the way towards Eileen's room. "You better go in first, you're the VSO."

Rachael nodded, "I've spoken to the boss about that."

"What about?"

"A secondment to the Major Investigation Team. If I got it, I could work more closely with Jane."

"Do you think he'll let you go?"

"I don't know, but I've asked." She knocked on the door before entering the room. "Hello, Eileen, it's Rachael and Mel here. Staff nurse says you're a bit better today. How are you feeling?"

"Blind, Rachael, it's very dark in here now."

"We met a Mr Donovan in the lift, is that your lawyer?"

"I don't know him, but Jamie said he'd see about getting me a lawyer, that's probably him. He's into personal injury. Jamie says his pop, Ian, knows him and he'll do a good job for me. Sue the dating agency and everything. Jamie says I'll get a packet, but I'd rather be able to see."

"I can understand that."

"Sorry, Mel, but you really can't."

"Jamie and Linda not here today?"

"Linda's coming up later. Jamie's working today. But he did phone for a chat."

"That's good," Rachael said. "Eileen, do you mind if Mel and I sit down, we'd like to go through everything you can remember about Frederick, again."

"Really? I told you all I can remember before."

"Please? Just in case we've missed anything or written something down wrongly. It would help us catch this bastard."

"Then let's do it. Could you pass me my orange juice, Rachael? I'll wet my whistle and we'll get going."

Mel and Rachael watched as Eileen wriggled to a more comfortable sitting position in her bed and took a sip of her drink.

"Where do you want me to start?"

"Perhaps with how you met."

"It was through a dating agency a work colleague found for me. She downloaded the app onto my phone." Eileen began to tell her story all over again.

"She's quite consistent. Everything she said yesterday matched with what she told us today, right down to the angle that the photo was taken to show him as having long legs and the golden Labrador dog," Mel said. "Personally, I prefer cats, but that's another matter."

"I wonder if he did that thing where most of what you say is true, so the lies are easier to remember."

"Like what?"

"Like living in North Berwick. Saying he lives with his cousin, rather than a brother. Telling her he lived in a fancy house on the outskirts of town instead of a converted flat that's part of what was a grand house."

"Like John Hamilton, who wouldn't know truth or a lie if it hit him in the face?"

"Just like that. Or he lives with his cousin in a fine house on the outskirts of a town, just not North Berwick."

"She did tell us one new thing today. That Frederick told her he was brought up by his uncle and his uncle was a vintner."

"Yes, that was new."

"Wasn't Felix Buchanan brought up by Lachlan's family?"

"How would I know that?"

"And although the late Earl wasn't a vintner, he did own a vineyard in Spain and another in Australia. He was very knowledgeable about wine, brandy and that sort of thing."

"How would you know?"

"When Tim and Bear get together with men they were at school with, they gossip like old women. I'll check with Bear, but I'm sure I remember him saying that."

"I didn't think he and Tim were at school with Lucky."

"They weren't. Lucky and Felix went to Fettes while Tim and Bear were at Merchiston Castle with Simon and Robin Land. But all around the same time. I think Felix and Robin are a bit younger, but not by much."

"So, they've known each other for a long time."

"Yes, and from what I know of Lucky and Felix, they wouldn't know how to tell the truth any better than John Hamilton. We know that Eileen met Frederick through a dating app. Do you think John would use a dating app?"

"I don't know. I wonder what John's brother's like," Rachael said.

"I hope he's not like John."

Rachael laughed. "I know what you mean. By the way, talking about bad boys, did you tell the boss about Jamie's shenanigans against his neighbour?"

"Fuck. I forgot. Remind me to type out a report when we get back to the station."

Hunter wandered into the incident room to find Tim in the corner making coffees and teas for the team. "Got any biscuits?"

"Jaffa cakes or hob nobs."

"You can't beat a hob nob," Hunter said as he picked a couple out of the tin.

"You just come in here to nick our biscuits, boss, or were you looking for me?"

"The latter. I've just got a report from Mel that Jamie Thomson is causing trouble with his neighbours."

"They're not going to hold the front page for that, boss. Jamie could cause an argument in an empty room."

"True enough. Apparently, the couple want to move, and he wants to speed them up so that he and Linda can move into the other half of Frankie's semi."

"I'd want to move if I lived next door to Jamie too. But where do I come in?"

"He held his hands up to letting a mouse loose in the porch. Frightened Mrs Morrison half to death." Hunter smiled. "But he claimed he didn't leave the dead cat on their doorstep."

"Dead cats don't sound like Jamie's style, boss."

"I didn't think so either. Then Charlie's got a report today that the couple's car has been keyed while it was sitting in their driveway and their living room window has been plastered with oil."

"No way Jamie would damage a car like that, boss," Tim said. "You want me to go and talk to him? I could try and find out what's really going on."

"Mel says he's working today. Swing round to Thomson's Top Cars on your way home and find out the lie of the land."

"That's a long way for a short cut, but I'll go."

. . .

"Hi Blondie, please tell me you want a new car. I'm dying here. We need the business, don't we Frankie?"

"Always. We'll even throw in a free spare tyre."

"Good try, but no new car today, Jamie. But I do want to talk about a car."

"Those bloody Morrisons, isn't it? Have they reported me? Bastards. How many times do I have to tell them? I didn't key their fucking car."

"Any idea who did?"

"Hold on a minute. Frankie, have you got our crystal ball, or did it get broke when we were playing marbles? I don't know, for fucks' sake man, get a grip." Jamie strode towards his office.

"Not so fast," Tim said. "You keep your ear to the ground. Your dad's in the big house and he heard the Morrisons want to move before their house goes on sale. Come on Jamie, what's happening? And did you grease their windows?"

Jamie grinned at Tim. "Look, I'll hold my hands up to messing their windows, but no way I damaged their car. I couldn't do a thing like that."

"No, I doubt you could."

"As to who else has it in for them, they've been in with Arjun Mansoor and his lot. If they've crossed him, or someone else on his behalf, they'll have a lot more than a keyed car to worry about and I'd want to move house fast if that was the case."

"Come on, Jamie, Arjun's still inside."

"So's my pop, but he still pulls the strings."

CHAPTER
TWENTY-FOUR

OSKAR SMILED AS HE PULLED THE WARRANT OUT OF THE ENVELOPE. This was a good start to his new post. He really hadn't been sure that they had enough to get one, but he'd heard about John Hamilton from Colin and laid all that information out in his documentation. He'd also been told about the North Berwick connection by Rachael and wove that into his petition to the court too. He was pleased with himself and hoped Hunter would be too. He bounded up the stairs two at a time to show off his success.

Nadia was speaking with Hunter. "Neither of them has come in yet, boss, but the girlfriend phoned to say John was with her all night and his cousin claims he was in the pub, mortal drunk because John had told him not to get back too early on pain of death," Nadia said. "To be honest, if they're anything like John, I'm not sure I believe either of them, but Hector's given me the name of the pub if you want me to stop in."

"Yes, do that, Nadia. Take Colin with you and see if they've got any CCTV that corroborates this guy's whereabouts. What's the brother's name again?"

"Hector, boss."

"Hector Hamilton? There's a name to conjure with. See what you can find out and let me know."

"Oskar, don't stand on ceremony, just come in, man." Hunter waved the new DI into his office and motioned for him to take a seat. "I can tell from the grin on your face that you got your warrant. Do we have powers to search the home as well as the office?"

"Yes, we do. It's a good start for me here."

"Excellent. Take a team of uniforms down and you and Mel can lead the search of the office. I'll get Bear and Neil into the house."

"You won't be there?"

"No, if it's you, it's someone neutral. If I'm there John can complain that I still bear a grudge from his time here."

"And do you?"

"Only because he brought the force into disrepute. We don't need that."

"Anything else you want me to be aware of?"

"Not really, but although the girlfriend and brother have phoned in, I still want to interview them sooner rather than later. You know, to see the whites of their eyes."

"You really want to use that phrase in this case?"

"Maybe not. Now get out of here and put your team together."

When Bear and Neil arrived at the flat John and Hector shared, they were surprised when a woman answered the door in a dressing gown. It wasn't a very feminine design so Bear thought it must belong to one of the brothers. She only opened the door a little way and peered round the side.

"What do you want? Why are all these coppers here? I've been on night shift, and I was just off to my kip."

"I'm sorry to disturb you," Bear said. "I was led to believe that John and Hector Hamilton live here. Is that not the case?"

"Aye, they do. I'm with John and I'm staying here now. What are you lot doing here?"

"You must be Katy," Neil said. "John mentioned you when I met him at his office. Are you alone in the flat?"

"Yes, I'm alone and I'm Katy, who the hell are you?"

"DC Neil Larkin and this is my colleague DC Winston Zewedu. We have a warrant to allow us to search these premises."

"You'll have to give me a minute to get dressed and tidy up. You can't come in with the place looking like this."

"I'm sorry, that won't be possible. We do require entry right now." Bear shoved the door open and instructed the uniforms to go in and search everywhere."

"But I've just had a shower, I'm not decent." The woman whined. "Give me a couple of minutes to get dressed in the bedroom."

"I can't leave you alone," Bear said. "But this woman PC will come into the bedroom with you, and you can get dressed."

"No way! How do I know she's not a dike just getting off on watching me?"

"You don't," the PC said. "But it's the best offer you're going to get and, if you don't want to be arrested and carted off to the station in that dressing gown, you better take it." She followed the woman into the bedroom and closed the door gently behind them.

"That's odd," Neil said.

"What?"

"John said his girlfriend worked in the office and showed houses and she said she's his girlfriend, but she was working night shift. I don't know any estate agents who work night shift, do you?"

"Interesting. No. Neil, I don't. Will you take the bathroom if I do the kitchen? The uniforms can search the living room and bedrooms."

Neil pulled on his blue latex gloves and started to look in every medicine bottle in the bathroom. He even took out the panel at the bottom of the little cupboard under the sink and was rewarded for his efforts with a sizeable plastic bag. The contents smelled like weed. He smiled and put his find into an evidence bag. There were also traces of powder on the lid of the cistern. Neil lifted that with tape so it could be examined.

Bear was equally thorough and delved into every box and container in the kitchen. He was almost sorry to find the finely ground contents of the container marked 'sugar' reacted like cocaine when he touched his tongue with a tiny amount. He looked at the quantity of the powder and wondered how John and Hector could afford so much coke. He must be sure to ask them.

In the living room, the team of uniformed officers found a large stash of cash in the drawer by the window, bagged it and marked it up. The female officer also found traces of a white powder on the dressing table in the room Katy shared with John. When she went to put tape over it, Katy blew it away."

"What you doing? That's just my make-up. You should try it; you'd look miles better."

The PC didn't reply but used the tape anyway. She knew the woman's breath wouldn't have removed every particle of whatever was there.

When Katy finished dressing, Bear told her that they needed her to come to the station to answer some questions.

"But I told you, I was on night shift. I'm knackered."

"You can have a sleep in the cells if you like, but I can't leave you here." Bear led the woman gently by the arm, out to one of the waiting cars. You sit in the back with her, will you, Neil?"

Oskar and Mel had as much difficulty parking as Nadia had had the previous day. Unfortunately, neither of them had her skill, so their walk to John's office was much longer.

Oskar checked the building before they entered to see if there were any other exits, but it appeared the only door was the one onto the main street. They walked in and were greeted by a young woman on reception who had a, golden labrador curled up at her feet.

"May I help you?" She asked Oskar.

"Yes, we're looking for John and Hector Hamilton. Are they in?"

She looked at her switchboard. John is on the phone, but Hector is free. Who shall I say is here?"

"DI Krol and DC Grant from Police Scotland."

"Gemma, can you put a call through to head office? Oh, hello, who have we here?" The man who was speaking was nearly six feet tall. He had regular features that gave his face a pleasing symmetry. However, it was his dark brown hair and full dark beard that first caught the officer's attention. Then he fixed his gaze on Oskar, held out his hand and said, "Hector Hamilton, how can I help?"

It was only then that Oskar noticed the man's dark brown eyes and long eyelashes. Those eyes are wasted on a man, he thought. He pulled out his ID and showed it to the man.

"Hello Mr. Hamilton, DI Oskar Krol and DC Grant. We're here to search your premises."

"I don't think so, what on earth would give you that right?"

"This warrant, sir. If you just sit there, we won't be long." Oskar indicated that Hector should sit in the reception area then quickly waved in the uniformed officers.

"I'll ask John to finish up his call," Gemma said.

"That won't be necessary, Miss." Mel flicked a switch on her exchange board. "See, all done. You sit over there beside your boss while I search your desk."

John came charging out of his room. "What the hell, Gemma." He looked around at the policemen walking in. "What the fuck is going on?" He caught sight of Mel and recognised her. "Mel, what are you lot doing here? God in heaven, haven't I suffered enough at the hands of bloody Hunter and his team?"

"The court thinks not. We are conducting a search in terms of this warrant," Mel said.

John snatched the document out of her hands.

"Fuck. This is for the office and the flat."

"Indeed, it is. Now if you sit over there beside your brother, we'll be as quick as we can," Oskar said.

"I'll need to phone my girlfriend, she's in the flat alone after her nightshift."

"You'll be too late," Oskar said. "Our colleagues will already be there. Don't worry, they'll introduce themselves."

Oskar moved into the small toilet to the left of reception and was almost disappointed not to find anything suspicious hidden in the cistern. Then he heard Mel shout to him.

"Oskar, you got an evidence bag?"

"Yes. Here. What have you found?"

"Money, I'm not sure how much, can you count it with me?"

"It's just a deposit a client left with us for their new house," John said.

"Surely in terms of the money laundering legislation, you shouldn't accept this much cash."

Mel and Oskar found the sum to be five pounds short of ten thousand pounds.

"That's a strange amount," Oskar said.

Both John and Hector looked at Gemma.

"I took a fiver to get the milk this morning." She whined.

"Very professional." Oskar labelled the evidence bag and put it away.

"I'm new."

"You're bloody fired." John growled.

"Boss, I've found this in the desk drawer." PC Scott Clark shouted from John's room. He held up a small bag of white powder.

"Old habits die hard, John," Mel said.

"Bag it and tag it. We'll send it to the lab," Oskar said. "Not enough to supply," he muttered to Mel.

"No bloody way that was in John's desk. Your boys planted that." Hector shouted. He stood up and lunged towards Oskar who deftly caught his wrist and wrenched it up his back. As they stood toe to toe, he whispered in Hector's ear. "Bad idea to attack a Pole who's trained to fight a Russian army," he said. "Mel, cuff him and we'll take these three into the station for questioning.

"What about the business?" John asked.

"I just got you a half day." Oskar replied.

Colin knocked on Hunter's door. He didn't wait for a reply before he walked in and told Hunter that John, his brother and receptionist had all been brought in for questioning.

"No," Hunter said.

"I haven't asked a question yet," Colin said.

"You are going to ask if you can interview John. I saved you the bother of saying it. You can interview the receptionist with Neil."

"Thanks a lot, boss."

CHAPTER TWENTY-FIVE

HUNTER STUCK HIS HEAD AROUND THE DOOR OF THE INCIDENT ROOM. He saw Tim sitting gazing into the middle distance instead of looking as if he were working.

"Young Myerscough," he said. "You are looking particularly unfocussed. Want to go for a ride?"

"I bet you say that to all the nice boys, boss." Rachael smiled.

"Maybe, but nobody ever said Tim was a nice boy."

Tim got up and followed Hunter towards the door. "Where are we going today?"

"We're off to the countryside to see Lachlan and Felix. I don't think I've ever met Felix."

"You've led a charmed life, boss. My car or a pool car?"

"No contest. Your car and you drive."

Tim nodded and followed Hunter to the car park. He unlocked the car from halfway across. "I take it we've heard back from the Spanish police. Is there a warrant out on Felix?"

"No, but there would have been if he hadn't left Ibiza so quickly. He was there for less than twenty-four hours."

"Yet he still managed to get into trouble. It must be a gift. Do we know what went on?"

"I'll tell you what the Spaniards said while we're on our way. I have a much more pressing problem."

"Can I help?"

"Not unless you can think of a good way for me to celebrate Gillian's birthday, before she leaves for Moscow."

"Injured young women aside, the Pompadour was lovely."

"A bit formal, perhaps."

"Then it's your problem."

"Thanks Boss. You're all heart."

When they got to Lachlan's estate, Hunter was surprised by the length of the driveway.

"It's quite a pile, isn't it?" He looked at grand house coming into view.

"Yes, the Buchanan's are an old family," Tim said.

"Doesn't make them better than the rest of us."

"Don't let Lucky hear you say that boss." Tim grinned and pulled up behind the Range Rover. "Well, it looks like Lucky's at home." He locked his car, out of habit, rather than necessity.

Hunter walked towards the door taking in his surroundings. He thought about his own modest flat in Leith and looked at the mansion in front of him. It did him no good to wonder why, and he wasn't jealous. You could only be in one room at any time, he just wondered why such disparities between rich and poor were allowed to continue today. Some folk struggled to make ends meet from one month to the next and others didn't know the end or beginning of their entitlement.

Oh dear, he was beginning to think like his father. They

would laugh about that at the next family dinner. He rang the bell and was aware of Tim standing behind him. He was another man who was so wealthy that he could probably buy this estate from under the Buchanans, but Tim rarely let that slip. He did his job, not for the money, but out of a sense of duty and because he loved it.

A man in a sharp suit answered the door. "How may I assist you, gentlemen?"

"DI Hunter Wilson and DC Tim Myerscough to see Lord Lachlan and Sir Felix Buchanan," Hunter said.

"Of course, sir. Mr Timothy, I didn't notice you there."

As Tim stood six foot four in his socks, Hunter thought this was unlikely, but made no comment."

"Good to see you, too, McKellar," Tim said.

"The gentlemen are in the library, just let me tell them you're here."

Hunter looked around the entrance hall. He felt glad he didn't have to clean and tidy this space before Meera stayed over. Then he thought that if he lived here, he'd have people to do that for him.

"This way detectives. Tea or coffee?"

"Coffee please," Hunter said.

"Thanks, McKellar, make that two," Tim said. He followed Hunter into the library and Lucky did the introductions.

"I believe you're here about that dreadful attack on the young woman at the Waldorf Astoria. Ghastly," Lucky said. "Of course, I was still in rehab and Felix was out of the country, so I don't see how we can help, but we will if we can. Anything for the boys in blue, right, Felix?"

"Yes, Lucky, anything at all. As long as it's not running. I had to run to catch my plane home and twisted my ankle. All strapped up, I'm afraid."

McKellar opened the door and a young woman brought in a tray with a large cafetiere and a plate of home-made biscuits on it.

"That's fine, thank you. We'll serve ourselves," Lucky said.

When all the drinks were poured and biscuits offered, Hunter returned to business.

"Lord Buchanan, can you tell us what your routine was at the end of your time in the rehabilitation facility?"

"The staff are good, but not trusting. Advisedly so," Lucky said. "There are cameras all over the grounds. You have to be careful, or they watch your every move."

"And were you?"

"What?"

"Were you careful?"

"Sometimes. But towards the end of your time, they want to know that you can be trusted in the outside world. That's the most difficult bit. I've always ridden, so I made use of the local riding stables. Sometimes they'd encourage me to go out for coffee or for a pub lunch. Probably just to see that I could do it without coming back high."

"Probably," Tim said.

"The dealers know the facility is there so there's always one ready to pounce or entice you back to the dark side."

"Did you succumb?" Tim asked.

"No. I rather surprised myself. I even gave up the fags for a while, but that was a step too far. Still, I'm training for a marathon, so I'd go running in the evenings. It's cooler then, I preferred to run in the evenings."

"Did you have a curfew?" Hunter asked.

"Not towards the end. You have to sign in and out but there's no curfew as such."

"The sign in book shows you were out on the evening of the attack," Tim said.

"I probably was. I don't remember specifically, but I was doing a lot of running then and still am."

"Can you think about that evening, Lord Buchanan? Did you see anybody while you were out? Or more specifically, would anybody have seen you?"

"Let me think. I remember there was a bit of a drizzle most evenings. Oh yes, and it was the day after Jessie's birthday."

"Who's Jessie?"

"A nurse at the facility, boss." Tim replied.

"I do remember it. I passed one woman who was out walking her dog. Some kind of fashionable half-breed with a silly name. A few cars drove past me and there was one car in a layby with a couple in it. My goodness how that one was rocking about. I doubt any of them would even have noticed me, especially that couple." Lucky snorted with laughter and glanced at Felix. He laughed too.

"The sign in book shows you got back quite late," Tim said. Theoretically, you could have had dinner in Edinburgh and got a taxi back to the rehab centre."

"Maybe I could have, but I didn't, Tim."

"Jessie said you grew your beard in rehab."

"But it didn't suit me, I shaved it off. Just kept the moustache and a bit of George Michael stubble. Looks good, don't you think?"

"You shaved it off the day you left. She mentioned it when I picked you up. Do you have contact lenses?"

"Yes, so what?"

"Could we see them please? All of them."

"What are you getting at now, Tim?"

"Lucky, you have blue eyes. We know our perpetrator had brown eyes."

"Then it wasn't me."

"Do you have any coloured contact lenses?"

They turned their attention to Felix, who looked around the room nervously. "I was away for just under a week at that time, so I can't really assist you gents."

"It's interesting because the Spanish authorities tell a different story," Hunter said. "They told us you arrived on the last flight onto Ibiza, did a DJ gig until the early hours and left the following morning before they could collar you for a complaint made by a local woman."

"That's not how I remember it. Anyway, does that mean they're not chasing me?"

"They're not, but I doubt you'll be welcome on the island any time soon. I hope the gig was worth it," Hunter said.

"Damn right it was. I made a fortune for four hours work. That bitch was an old tart anyway."

"You seemed to like her enough to bite and scratch her and rip her clothes."

"If that's what she said, she's a liar. Anyway, I couldn't have attacked your woman, I wasn't here."

"If you came back so soon, why did it take you so long to get in touch with me and come home?" Lucky asked.

"Things to do, man. You know how it is."

"It would have been tight, but there's just about enough time for you to be our man,"

"That's ridiculous. No way I'd have made my flight."

"Felix, witnesses have identified you and with brown eyes and dark hair and beard, I'm afraid you're in the frame," Tim said.

"Are Lucky and I under arrest?"

"No, but don't go anywhere, will you? Thanks for the coffee." Hunter stood up and he and Tim left the men together in the library.

CHAPTER TWENTY-SIX

"Hunter. Hunter, we've had a call about a burglary in West Mains Road. It's a Mr Morrison who's reported it. Says your lot have been in touch with his neighbour, Jamie Thomson. He and Thomson don't get along and he's sure Thomson has instigated this break-in today," the desk sergeant said.

"I don't suppose he has any evidence, Charlie?"

"What, beyond Jamie Thomson being a troublesome arse? No, I don't think he does. Do you want to send someone over to work with my boys?"

"I'll send Myerscough and Grant over, Charlie. They've dealt with Jamie Thomson and his family before."

"Fucks sake, Hunter, we've all dealt with the bloody Thomsons. Fine, I'll tell them Myerscough and Grant are on their way."

Tim pulled up behind the panda car and walked towards the Morrison's home.

"Aren't we here to question Jamie?" Mel asked.

"Yes, but I'd like to know what we're questioning him about before we knock on his door."

"Good thinking. Have you decided what to do for Gillian's birthday yet?"

"I haven't done that much thinking."

They put on their protective gear at the gate then went into the Morrison's house. Mrs Morrison was sitting on the stairs crying. Mr Morrison was shouting at PC Scott Clark while photographer Sam Hutchins quietly got on with her job taking pictures of everything as it had been found.

"CSIs on their way, Scott?" Mel asked.

"They're here already. In the dining room just now, I think."

Mr Morrison continued bellowing and Tim had had enough. He pulled himself up to his full height and looked down at the irate man.

"How dare you speak to my colleague like that, Mr. Morrison? You need his help. You need my help. And you are not going to get it tonight if you do not calm down. I suggest that you go into the hallway and comfort your wife. Then, it might be nice to check how everybody takes their tea and boil a kettle. Do I make myself clear?"

"But that little fucker Jamie has gone too far this time. All me valuables are gone. He's taken the lot. Even the things in the safe under the floorboards in the dining room. He knows I'm waiting to get my hip done, so I can't give chase, can I? He's a bloody parasite, that boy."

"You don't know it was Jamie Thomson and neither do I. Let us do our job while you comfort your wife." Tim paused and then said. "Did Jamie know about your safe under the floor?"

"Doubt it. How would he? He's only been in once or twice and never for dinner."

"That's what I thought. Who did know about the safe?"

"I don't know. My nephew, he advised us to put it in. It wouldn't be him, he's family. Arjun, but he's inside."

"Arjun Mansoor?"

"Yes, he's a family friend."

"Mr Morrison, Arjun Mansoor is nobody's friend. What's your nephew's name?"

"Hector. Hector Hamilton. He's done right well for himself. Estate agent down the coast, he is. His brother John works with him too, now. Great lads."

"I see. We'll do our best by you and your wife and try to find out who invaded your home. Mine's just milk, thanks."

"Scott, you okay here?"

"Yeh. It'll be fine. You going next door?"

"We'll go and speak to Jamie, now."

Tim and Mel rang the doorbell of Jamie's home that he and Linda shared with Frankie and his family. Frankie opened the door. He had a plastic fork in one hand and a plate of chicken nuggets and peas in the other.

"Come in. You look all kitted out for a fancy dress party," he said. "It's time for the girls to eat and you don't want to get between Kylie or Dannii and their food."

Tim and Mel followed him into the dining room where Donna was supervising Kylie, and Dannii was clearly relieved to see her father return with her plate.

"We're looking for Jamie," Mel said. "Is he in?"

"No, he and Linda have been at the hospital all day. Eileen's having difficulty coming to terms with being blind and all three of them had time with folk form the Royal National Institute of Blind People, Guide Dog people, Sight Scotland and all sorts of therapists. I think someone was going in from Eileen's work too, just to reassure her that they want her back."

"That seems a lot in one day."

"I said that, Mel. But when did Jamie ever listen to me, or anybody else for that matter? Is this about the break-in next door? Because we can't help you much, Donna and I were at Thomson's Top Cars all day. You can check our CCTV, if you want."

"Thanks Frankie, we'll get a uniform over tomorrow to pick it up. I suppose the staff in the ward and the hospital CCTV will tell us Jamie was where you say he was too," Tim said. "Do you know where Mr and Mrs Morrison kept their valuables?"

"In the wardrobe? A drawer in the dressing table? Under the bed?" Frankie suggested.

"Some people keep stuff in their mattress." Donna volunteered.

"Do they?"

"You have both done very well girls. Would you like a yoghurt?"

The girls clamoured for the suggested treat and Frankie grinned.

"Is that it?" he asked Tim.

"Yes, thanks Frankie, we'll see ourselves out."

CHAPTER
TWENTY-SEVEN

When Tim and Mel closed the door from Frankie and Jamie's home, they heard Mr. Morrison bellowing again. This time the CSIs seemed to be in the line of fire. Tim was reaching the end of his patience and jumped the fence between the gardens to come face to face with the man.

"Mr. Morrison, you're shouting at my colleagues again. I told you not to do that."

"They want to take fingerprints from me and my wife. That's not right. They'll add them to a secret database that the government is keeping."

"Believe me, that is not so."

"Then why do they need them, huh? Of course our fingerprints are going to be in our house. We bloody live here."

Tim took a deep breath. "Exactly. If we have a record of your prints and we find them around where your valuables are kept, we can discount them from our enquiries and find the thieves more quickly. If we don't have your fingerprints, everything takes longer because we have to check and discount you and Mrs Morrison every time we find them."

"And what happens to them later?"

"We destroy them. We no longer need them for elimination purposes once your case is completed."

"And that's true?"

"That's true."

"Maggie, give them your prints doll, it'll let them catch that little turd next door faster."

Tim shook his head and went to speak to Chloe who led the CSIs. He learned they had found several sets of prints that they would have to send off for identification. There was also the safe under the floor in the dining room that had been opened and the contents taken but the one under the kitchen floor hadn't been touched.

"What's in that one?" Tim asked.

"No idea. Mr Morrison refuses to open it. He says it's not relevant because it only has documents in it," Sam said. "He won't let me go up into the loft either. Says nobody's been up there and nothing is taken."

"How does he know if no one has looked?" Sam shrugged and carried on with her work. The CSIs looked equally bemused.

"Mr Morrison," Tim said.

"In the kitchen getting me prints done lad."

"Why do you think the safe under the kitchen floor wasn't touched?"

"Nobody knew it was there. Only me and Maggie."

"What's in it?"

"Copies of our Wills, titles for the house that kind of gubbins. Nowt that'll sell."

"Can we check your attic, in case that's how the burglars got in?"

"Me door was busted, lad. That's how they got in. That's all about it."

"That's fine, but any crime number we give you will exclude the attic because we haven't had a chance to check it. Your insurance company will notice that."

"Fuck."

CHAPTER TWENTY-EIGHT

"So, you never got to speak to Jamie?" Hunter asked Mel.

"No, boss, he was still at the hospital with Eileen and Linda. The staff confirmed they'd been in and out of meetings and therapy sessions all day right from early doors."

"I think I'd need more than therapy if I'd been through what Eileen's suffered. Still, I'd like you to talk to Jamie about the burglary at the Morrisons. Catch up with him today, will you, Mel? And if Neil's going to work with our team, he might as well get to know Jamie Thomson too. He'll see enough of him. Why is that lad at the centre of anything that goes wrong in this city?"

Mel and Neil arrived early at Jamie's West Mains Road home. He answered the door holding a piece of jammy toast in his left hand.

"Mel, darlin' couldn't even get past breakfast without thinking about me, could you?" He grinned. "Come in. I don't think I know your pal."

"DC Neil Larkin," Mel said.

"Milk no sugar. Am I right? How do you take your tea, Neil?"

Mel couldn't help smiling at Jamie's cheek. She followed him into the large living-dining room and introduced the family to Neil. Then she and Neil sat down on the over-sized leather settee and waited while Jamie poured their tea.

"Bonny girls," Neil said. "How old are they?"

"Almost three, they'll be having a birthday party soon with cake."

"Cake, cake." Kylie and Dannii squealed and rubbed their tummies.

"Where does their red hair come from?"

"Their Mum. Annie was beautiful."

Mel was ruing the fact she was too far from Neil to kick him. And, for once, was glad that Jamie came back into the room. He was carrying their tea. He handed it out and then sat back at the dining table to finish his breakfast. Before he shovelled a forkful of food into his face he spoke again to Mel.

"You'll be here about the burglary next door. The old bastard will be blaming me. But you can't fit me up for that one."

"I don't want to fit you up for anything, Jamie. However, your fingerprints have been found all around the house. They were even found on the hasp securing the attic."

"Mel, I'm not surprised. I fitted the fucking hasp. Before we fell out with the Morrisons I even fixed their car. No charge mind, and that's my business. Old Ma Morrison invited me in for a cuppa to say thanks, but the old man gave me a beer."

"When did you fall out?" Neil asked.

"We'll get to that bit. He doesn't like a proper story, that one, does he?" Jamie asked Mel.

"None of us do, but some of us have learned to live with it. Go on."

"Well, I had to go upstairs to the loo, and I went into the wrong room."

"How did you manage that? The house is the mirror image of yours."

"That's it, mirror image. But I did see a lot of paperwork in the little bedroom."

"What for?"

"I don't know, but all sorts of names and addresses. Colour coded they were. Odd. But I couldn't linger because the old man was shouting up if there was enough paper in the bog."

Mel watched Neil pull a face and thought he'd have to get used to worse stories than that if he were to make it in Hunter's team.

"Anyway, they're pally with Arjun. And you know where that gets you, Mel." Frankie added.

"But Arjun Mansoor's inside," Neil said.

Jamie snorted. "Your pal's got a lot to learn. Next he'll be telling me there's no drugs or mobile phones inside."

Mel shrugged. "That's not our domain. But how come your fingerprints were still in the house. It must have been a while back that you were still on good terms with the Morrisons."

"It is. Just shows what a dirty old devil she is. Should have cleaned better. And you can't get me for yesterday. Linda and I were up at the hospital with Eileen all day. We met with the Blind Society people, folk for Guide dogs and her work popped in to say they want her back."

"That must have been good for Eileen," Mel said.

"Yes, but tiring. I was exhausted so she must have been right knackered," Linda said.

"They had therapists in too and we had to stay so we can learn what they do to help her, and we can do it too. Lots to think about. Anyway, the nurses can tell you we were there."

"They did, and the hospital CCTV confirmed it. But can you think who might have wanted to break into the Morrisons' home?"

"Look, their nephew is that former copper and they work with Arjun Mansoor, go talk to them."

"We will, Jamie."

"In the meantime, have you got the bastard who blinded poor Eileen? That's got to be more important than a few baubles nicked from our neighbours."

"We have a few suspects and are interviewing them," Neil said.

"Yap yap yap. Good for you. Give me a few names and I'll get a fucking confession for you."

"That won't help, Jamie. We'll find him," Mel said. "Thanks for the tea. We better go."

"It may not help you, but it'll make me feel a lot better. Just as well pop's on the case."

"Tell your dad not to blot his copy book this time. Leave it to us."

"Great idea, Mel. That'll work."

The change of tone in Jamie's voice frightened the twins and Kylie and Dannii burst into tears, holding their arms up to their father. Frankie gathered them up, one in each arm.

"Nice one, Jamie. It's not the girls' fault," he said. "If you've asked all your questions, you and your pal can just go, DC

Grant. Or if you need to talk to Jamie more, do it somewhere else."

"No, I think we can go. Jamie has explained why his fingerprints are in the Morrisons' house. Sorry for disturbing you, and the girls, Frankie."

"Mel, I don't want to see any of you plods until you've got Eileen's attacker locked up and the key has been well and truly thrown away. That clear?" Jamie asked. "There's the door. Go get 'im Mel. Get him before I do."

"Do you believe him?" Hunter asked Mel and Neil.

"He was certainly adamant," Neil said.

"You know Jamie, boss, he can be adamant whether he's guilty or innocent," Mel said. "But this time he invited us to check with the hospital staff and the CCTV. He was also clear as to why his prints were in various parts of his neighbours' home. To be honest, boss, this time I believe him."

"Yes, I'm inclined to believe him too. And I don't like this connection between the Morrisons and Mansoor. I think I'll ask Colin and Nadia to get over to Saughton and interview him at HMP Edinburgh because we've identified his prints in the house too. You two get your reports written up."

CHAPTER TWENTY-NINE

"ARJUN'S A POPULAR GUY RIGHT NOW," THE GUARD SAID TO COLIN. "What's going on? Don't tell me, it's just a routine enquiry, right? Except nothing with Arjun is ever routine. We know that as well as you do. Right, I'll buzz you in and we'll get it organised."

Neither Colin nor Nadia commented on these observations, nor the running commentary the guard continued while they were subjected to the usual searches and put their valuables into lockers.

"You know Mansoor is one bad lot, he's in here for drugs and stuff, but I think he's still Mr. Big outside these walls too, you know? He's got all these cons dancing to his tune in here and as they get out, one by one, I'm sure they're on a mission for him. You know how it is. They get out, do his bidding and they're back in here so fast they've no time to settle to life in the real world, you know?" He paused for breath. "Anyway, you're clean. Just go through there to the waiting room. You know the way."

They sat in silence in the waiting room with the few others

who were waiting for admission. One woman in a suit was probably a lawyer, Colin thought while the young woman with the baby was probably the partner of a first timer on a compassionate visit.

The woman and baby were called through first. Colin looked at the guard. But got nothing back. Maybe he was in the huff because Colin and Nadia hadn't returned his chat. Colin really hoped that Arjun wasn't being difficult; that was the other possibility. Prisoners were permitted to change into their own clothes for visits, but few bothered for the police they saw as being responsible for their stay at Her Majesty's Prison. His hopes were rewarded. They and the suited woman were called through to undertake their respective visits in private rooms. Private, but a prison officer was stationed outside the door.

He watched as Arjun walked in and took the seat opposite himself and Nadia.

"A Chink? When did they get a Chinky copper in Edinburgh?"

Colin followed Nadia's lead and ignored the racist comment. Colin took the lead in the interview.

"Thank you for meeting with us Mr Mansoor."

"It's the most interesting thing that's going to happen today. Might as well."

"It's about your friends Mr and Mrs Morrison of West Mains Road. Their home was burgled last night."

"Well, it wasn't me. I was tucked up here. Ask anybody."

"I appreciate that Mr. Mansoor, but your fingerprints were found on the safe that was raided. It was under the floor in the dining room. Do you know why that would be?"

"Yes, probably because I put it in for them. It was

suggested to them for security by a relative, I think. They needed help securing it."

"Have you any idea what the Morrisons kept in it?"

"Not a clue." He laughed a forced, laugh devoid of humour. "I didn't stay around that long, just helped them put it in. They're not good company, the Morrisons."

"What makes you say that?" Nadia asked.

"They're dull, unimaginative, but I like to keep them sweet, they live next door to Ian Thomson's lad, so they can be useful."

"They may be dull, but you stayed around long enough for your prints to be on the door handle to the smallest bedroom."

"Perhaps I needed to use the facilities and mixed up my directions. I don't remember. It might be a good idea to speak to their relative or others who would know about the safe. Perhaps those who are not in jail." Mansoor stood up and left the room. The police officers had been dismissed.

Nadia drove them back to the station.

"Chink? How dare he! He's a bloody Paki." She exploded.

"I think he's of Kurdish extraction, actually. But I thought you handled it well and most professionally. Congratulations."

"Thanks, I think. You going to Tim's surprise dinner for Gillian's birthday?"

"No, Maggie's out at her pilates class, so I'm sitting in with the kids tonight. You?"

"No, it's Mum and Dad's wedding anniversary. We're having a family meal."

"Chinese?"

"What else?" she laughed.

. . .

Tim was pleased with himself. He had managed to arrange a birthday celebration for Gillian without her being aware of it. He texted Kenneth, one of the few members of staff his father still retained, to make sure he would remember to pick up Bear and Mel, Rachael and her wife Jane, then he and Gillian set off in his Mercedes to drive to the Longniddry Inn.

"You look beautiful tonight, Gillian. That is such a pretty outfit."

"Why thank you, Tim. You would think so, you bought it for me."

"But you chose it. The colour really suits you."

"Thank you, dear. I've always liked green. Maybe it's my Irish roots. Isn't it lovely to have a quiet dinner just the two of us, but are you sure you don't mind driving? I mean, Kenneth could drive us, and you could have a beer," Gillian said.

"Don't worry, pet. I thought this would be nice."

"It will, I love the Longniddry Inn, it's got a great ambience and the food is delicious."

When they arrived, he walked in front of her towards the restaurant. Kenneth had parked the car down a side street as he had asked, and it was only when he held the door open for Gillian that she saw their friends and heard them shout 'Surprise' that she realised it was going to be a bigger celebration.

She looked up at Tim and smiled. "Okay, you win. I didn't see this coming, but that's why Kenneth couldn't drive us, isn't it?"

"It is, Miss, yes." She turned round and saw Kenneth eating at the small table behind them. She bent down and kissed him on the cheek.

"Do you want to join us?" she asked.

"Sit down to dinner with you noisy young people. No thank you, Miss. There's little I would like less."

"Come on, let's get over to the group, Gillian" Tim said. "Thank you, Kenneth."

Conversation flowed freely and the guests all had presents for the birthday girl. Tim noticed that Bear had carried out his threat to give Gillian an English-Russian dictionary, although her Russian was fluent. She took the gift in good spirits, but Tim was pleased when Mel tempered that with a pretty cashmere scarf and hat, to ward against the eastern winds. Rachael and Jane had chosen a smart new briefcase for Gillian.

"Like getting a new school bag for my first day at school," she said.

"Oh dear, we forgot a new pencil case." Rachael laughed.

When the starters arrived, Tim asked if anybody wanted another drink. Bear and Rachael ordered more beer while it was agreed an extra bottle of white wine was needed for the table. Tim was only halfway through his pint of coke, so didn't order anything.

Just then, Tim felt a hand on his shoulder.

"Big celebration, is it?" John Hamilton asked. He and his brother Hector had walked in and noticed the table full of John's former colleagues.

"What are you doing here?" Bear asked.

"Out on bail, but hush, we're meeting business acquaintances. Arranging the party next month for being in business five years."

"At the moment, I'd suggest that might be a bit previous," Tim said. "When are you back for questioning?"

"Don't worry. We've got an appointment to be back at the station for ten tomorrow morning. Anyway, what are we celebrating here?"

"My birthday," Gillian said. She looked up at John and Hector. "Look at the lovely hat Mel got for me."

"That is beautiful," John said.

"And so are your eyes." Hector added. "I have never seen such bright green eyes ever. That hat shows them off perfectly. I like that flash of colour in your hair. Great idea."

"Thanks," Gillian said.

"Well, we'll meet again tomorrow. Have a good evening all of you," John said.

"We must get back to our guests, although I would much rather stay and stare into your eyes." Hector smiled and kissed Gillian on the cheek. "Happy birthday, darling," he said.

CHAPTER
THIRTY

HUNTER HAD AN EARLY MEETING WITH OSKAR. HE EXPLAINED THAT Neil had only recently been seconded to their team and checked that he would be happy interviewing John and Hector with Neil. He went on to explain that they were amongst the few members of the team who had not been working there when John was on the force.

He looked at the Pole and sipped his coffee as he waited for an answer. He watched as Oskar ran his hand through his thick, dark blond hair. The man's brow ruffled, and he broke into a smile that emphasised the creases around his blue eyes.

"You know, Hunter, you run this team very differently from others I have experienced. Never before has a senior officer asked my opinion on anything, never mind something as important as that."

"I'm not senior, Oskar. Just acting up."

"Oh, I've known a great many DCIs who have acted up," the Pole said. He smiled again. "But I mean it as a compliment," he said. "Anyway, I think it is a good idea that Neil and I interview the brothers. After all, he and I were involved in the search of the flat and office respectively."

"That's what I was thinking. We let them out on bail, but they're due back here tomorrow morning. I'd like to know if they can also explain how Hector's prints were found in that house that was burgled. It'll be interesting if their explanation matches that given by the victims. Also make sure you ask if they've ever used a dating app, will you?"

"What?"

"A dating website operated by an app on your phone. Just remember to ask, will you?"

"I'll try."

Oskar arrived early the following morning and took time to have a chat with Neil. As Neil was less used to interviewing, Oskar suggested that he lead the questioning and played bad cop, while Neil could take notes and interject at times to make helpful suggestions as the good cop.

He was pleased that Neil agreed to this arrangement because he didn't have a back-up plan. He took time to read the reports of the finds in both the flat and the office. The one that surprised him the most was the large amount of cash found in the office. That was such a rookie error.

Neil popped in to say that John and Hector had arrived, with their lawyer. Oskar looked at his watch. Ten minutes early. Good move.

"If I forget to ask, will you check if they've ever used a dating app?"

"That's a bit random, but yes, if you like."

"Thanks. Which interview room is free, Neil?"

"One is free and it's the biggest. Let's nab that before anybody else does."

"Good idea. Show John and the lawyer in there. We'll let them sit for a few minutes. Hector can wait in reception."

Neil was interested by John's reaction when he looked around the room. "You've not had the decorators in since I was last here," he said.

The room was small and dark. The only window had bars across it and was almost at the height of the ceiling. They couldn't see out of it. The bars were joined together by big, thick cobwebs. John's lip curled in disgust. He had clearly forgotten just how nasty these places were and the smell in the small rooms was never fresh. It didn't matter how much disinfectant the cleaners used or how much air-freshener the officers sprayed around after the rooms were used. Interview rooms always smelled of dirt, body odour and farts. This room was no different.

Neil held the door open for the young PC who would guard it and then left, closing the door quietly. He waited outside until Oskar came along.

"Still ready for good cop, bad cop?" the DI asked.

"Yes, and I'm all set to take notes too."

"Good, we'll start with the flat, then the office, then ask about the fingerprints at Morrisons' house."

"I thought that was just Hector's?"

"True, but I want to see what John says."

Neil smiled. "Ready when you are, sir." He opened the door and they walked in.

"Good morning, Mr Hamilton. Thank you for attending here today," Oskar said.

"It wasn't exactly an invitation that could be declined. Do you know my lawyer, Andrew Barley?"

"Only by reputation." Oskar introduced himself and he and Barley shook hands. Then the questioning began.

"John, a supply of marijuana was found in the bathroom in your flat. Does that belong to you?"

"I couldn't say. I wasn't there when it was uncovered. My guess is it was planted by one of your men who dislikes me."

"That seems unlikely. The weed is valued at over three thousand pounds. Few members of Police Scotland could afford that. Especially not just to harm someone they did not like.

"It was hidden in the bottom of the cupboard under the sink. Your fingerprints and those of one other person were found on the bag. Are you dealing, John?"

"Me? Who? No, never have. Succumbed to a little weed and snow now and then, but never a dealer."

"Who has access to your bathroom in the flat, John?" Neil asked.

"Funny you should ask that. Anybody who comes in. Anyone could have put it there. Maybe my fingerprints got onto the bag when I was looking out a new bar of soap."

"Who has been in your flat recently?" Oskar asked. "Say over the last month."

"Only me, Katy, and Hector. Oh, and the birds he's knocked about with. He's not got anyone special just now. Maybe one of them left it."

"I wouldn't leave gear worth that much money in the home of a casual acquaintance. Would you, John? I'd need to know I could get in and take it back," Oskar said.

"Well then, I can't help you. I don't know."

"I think my client has answered as much as he can about the marijuana allegedly found in his flat, don't you, Inspector?"

"There's no allegedly about it, Mr Barley. It was found hidden there. But let's move on.

"John, there was a large amount of cocaine found in your kitchen in a container marked 'sugar'. Is that yours? You have admitted to using cocaine. Do you deal to allow you to feed your habit?"

"I don't need to. I've got a good job. I bet I earn a lot more than you do."

"Maybe. But is the cocaine we found yours?"

"Of course not."

"Then who keeps their supply of cocaine in the sugar container of your flat? Is that another of Hector's female acquaintances?" Oskar asked.

"Perhaps your dealer forced you to hold on to it for them." Neil suggested.

"I don't know," John said.

"Then we'll move on," Oskar said. "Why did your girlfriend tell us she was just finished off a nightshift, but you told us she worked at your office as an estate agent?"

"For fuck's sake, what difference does that make? She doesn't work with us, she's a croupier at a casino. I thought it sounded better if I said she worked with us."

"At last, an answer that makes sense. Do you like to gamble, John?"

"Now and then. So what?"

"Moving on. A small quantity of cocaine was found in your desk in the office. "Is that yours."

"Yes. I had a little left over from the weekend. Enough for one cut."

"Thank you. Now there was a disturbingly large amount of cash found in the reception desk of your office. Almost ten thousand pounds. How did it get there?"

"A client paid a deposit; another paid a bill and the rest of it was our petty. None of the single amounts big enough to need a money laundering explanation."

"Interesting. That's not what I was told when we found it. No doubt your accounts will confirm what you say."

"I don't know. I don't keep the accounts. Hector does that."

"You don't seem to know very much, John. Do you know how Hector's fingerprints got on to the safe under the dining room floor in your uncle's home?"

"No. Ask Hector."

"We will. Just one last thing. Have you ever used the services of a dating agency?" Neil asked.

"What if I have? What's that got to do with anything? It's none of your business. Is it Mr Barley?"

"It does seem unconnected. Is there something on your mind we should know about, detective?"

Oskar arranged for John to be taken to wait in reception while Hector was brought through to the interview room. Barley took the opportunity for a break too. He told Oskar that he needed a fag and a pee because he wasn't as young as he used to be. Oskar agreed that it would be fifteen minutes before questioning of Hector commenced.

. . .

Hector had never been in a police interview room before. He was horrified by how musty it was. It made him gag. The tables and chairs were metal and bolted to the floor. There was a recording device on the table and that was bolted on to it and high on the wall was a camera. He stared at it. Could somebody see him now, he wondered.

There was a policewoman by the door. Hector looked at her and thought in other circumstances he might have had a shot at her. She was quite pretty. He moved around on his seat to see the wall behind him. The only window was there, but it was too high up to see out of it and it had bars in front of it. And the cobwebs. He had never seen any that thick. They seemed to form a net curtain over the window. This place smelt bad too. He gagged again and sat with his head in his hands until Andrew Barley came back into the room.

Oskar and Neil walked back in shortly afterwards and thanked Hector for his attendance.

"I just want to get things sorted," he said. "Ask me anything you want. I'll tell you the truth."

Oskar thought he was planning to ask what he wanted and that it would be a refreshing change to get honest replies, but he didn't say so. He asked Hector about the weed in the cupboard in the bathroom.

"I don't know if it's John's or Katy's, but I know it's not mine. I don't do drugs."

"John seemed to think it might have been left there by a friend of yours. Could that be right?" Neil asked.

"Unlikely. I rarely bring anybody back there. John and Katy make such exhibitions of themselves, you never know what you'll witness. I wish he'd get his own place."

"What about the cocaine we found in the sugar container in the kitchen, is that yours?" Oskar asked.

"Bloody hell, not again. I've told him I don't want that stuff in the house. You have extremely blue eyes, Inspector. It's rare to see such a distinctive colour."

"Indeed. Now John has admitted that the small amount of cocaine found in his desk at the office was his, but he was a little vague about how the ten thousand pounds came to be in the desk at reception. Can you help us with that?"

"A client wanted to pay a deposit in cash, but I said we couldn't take that much without knowing where it came from. He left it with us while he went to get a certificate from his accountant."

"Interesting, that's not what John said. And an accountant's certificate wouldn't be enough for your professional money laundering requirements, would it?" Oskar asked.

"Maybe not. I was trying to accommodate a good client."

"Another thing, Hector. You have an aunt and uncle in West Mains Road in Edinburgh."

"Not for much longer, they want to move house, I've been in measuring up and giving them advice quite recently. Their neighbours are ghastly."

"Your fingerprints were found on a safe under their dining room floor. How would they have got there?" Oskar asked.

"I put it in for them. The old man's a bit fingers and thumbs now. They keep stuff in it for a friend, I think."

"A friend? Who would that be?"

"It's a funny name, I'd never heard it before, Marshmallow or something."

"Mansoor?"

"That's it, I think."

"Fine, lastly, have you ever used a dating app?" Neil asked.

"You think I'd need to use a dating app? Look at this face, this physique."

"Even if you don't need to, have you ever done it?"

"Don't make me laugh."

CHAPTER THIRTY-ONE

HUNTER ARRIVED AT THE STATION EVEN EARLIER THAN USUAL, BUT Charlie was already in place behind reception.

"Morning Hunter. Do you know it's only nineteen pay checks until I retire?" the sergeant said.

"Best news I've had in a while, Charlie. But what will you do when you have all that time on your hands?"

"Easy, me and the wife are getting a motor home with my lump sum from my pension, and we'll travel the length and breadth of this green and pleasant land."

"That's sounds good. I might join you."

"Over my dead body. And speaking of which, a couple of reports came in from your fancy woman. I got Scott to put them on your desk."

Hunter nodded in response and climbed the stairs to his office. He set up his coffee machine and glanced at the reports. Meera had told him that the post-mortem reports on both the attacker's earlier victims should be with him today, along with her comments on Eileen. True to her word, all three were there.

He waited until he was able to pour his first coffee and then sat down to study the details.

First, he read through the post-mortem reports. Both women were white, single and looking for relationships on a new dating app that had been established in the USA for a while, but only recently moved its franchise to the UK as well. They were both a bit older than Eileen, but he didn't feel age was the factor for this man. He guessed that both women were lonely and vulnerable, as Eileen had been.

Why did he feel guilty that he and Meera had been able to save Eileen's life?

He turned his attention back to the first report. The woman who had been attacked in the woods near Ravelston had suffered a blow to the head. Meera thought a log or thick stick had been used because traces of moss and bark had been found around the wound. But her report indicated that this assault, although it would have stunned the victim, had not immediately led to her death.

She had also been drugged. Traces of the date rape drug Rohypnol had been found in her blood. Although Hunter was well aware of the effects of the drug, Meera had stated the relevant effects in her report because it was important that the whole team were fully aware that Rohypnol was a tranquiliser, much stronger than Valium and that, although it started working after twenty to thirty minutes, its strongest effects were usually felt within two hours of taking the drug and could continue for up to twelve hours. Bearing in mind the amount of Rohypnol found in this victim's body, it was likely that she would have been seriously incapacitated.

Meera had found a print-out from a dating website in the

woman's pocket. She had been matched with a man called Frederick. That was the name Eileen had whispered to Meera before they reached the hospital. Meera's report indicated that she didn't think this was a coincidence.

She also deduced that it was quite likely, bearing in mind the removal of the woman's eyes, that she had lain on the ground with her eyes open, able to observe her attacker and the events that led to her blindness, but was unable to move.

Hunter shuddered. That was disgusting. What a terrifying end of life experience. He was almost glad to read that, even if she had lived, the woman would have been unlikely to remember fully what happened because of the amount of the date rape drug found in her body.

He stared out of the window and noticed the sun breaking through. Eileen Maguire would never enjoy the sight of that again. Hunter poured himself another strong coffee and finished reading the report. It stated that the likely cause of death was a combination of shock to the body resulting from the crude removal of the eyes from their sockets, blood loss and hypothermia. Hunter found himself nodding as he read this. The woman had been found in Edinburgh in January, the whole area and especially the grounds of the woodlands where she was found would certainly have been cold and wet, and if she could move, she had no way to protect herself from the wind.

Hunter sighed and picked up the second report. It was much the same as the first, except that the woman had been found on a beach and the implement used to stun her by knocking her over the head appeared to have been a rock or a stone. Meera's report mentioned that in the wound at the back of her head she had found sand and traces of seaweed. Again, Rohypnol had been in her system. The removal of the woman's eyes would have been relatively unhindered by her inability to struggle or move after the drug had been administered. Hunter was depressed to note that the causes of death were the same for this woman as for the first victim who had been found.

Then he turned to a shorter report. Meera had spoken to Eileen and asked her if she would allow the hospital to release her medical notes to Meera so that she could compare Eileen's injuries with those of the other victims. Meera stated at the beginning of her notes that Eileen had consented, on the grounds that Meera thought it would help catch her attacker. Hunter felt grateful to this brave young woman who had suffered such a devastating loss.

He read on. Eileen's experience appeared to differ a little from those of the other women in that she had not been hit from behind to stun her. Perhaps her attacker had become more confident in his use of Rohypnol, and it had probably been administered earlier than it had to the other victims. Meera deduced this because Eileen remembered having to go to the ladies' room but had found herself dizzy and disoriented on her way there and back.

However, Eileen had been held in such a way that there were marks around her neck. Meera's notes suggested that she had been held in an upright position for the removal of her eyes because the lift was too small for her to lie down and give the attacker easy access. Meera also stated that Eileen's medical notes indicated that, but for the fact that she had been found so soon, Eileen would also probably have lost her life. The medical team at the hospital had ensured that she received fluids and bloods immediately to prevent her from going deeper into shock and to avoid her blood pressure crashing. They also quickly commenced the operation to cauterise her wounds and stop the bleeding and tidy up the site of the attack to avoid further blood loss and ensure she suffered as little pain as possible. The surgeons stated the condition of her eye sockets had been appalling. It was as if someone had used a serrated knife, like a steak knife, to harvest the eyeballs.

Hunter turned over the page. Looking at a blank sheet of paper for a few moments was quite comforting. Then he switched on his computer. The report from the CSIs about Jamie's neighbours was the first thing he saw in his in-box. That was all he needed.

He opened the email and read the numbered points. He would study it in more detail later.

1. Fingerprints found on the site included Jamie Thomson, John Hamilton, Hector Hamilton, Arjun Mansoor and Sir Felix Buchanan.
2. It looked as if someone wearing latex gloves had also been in the property as areas with otherwise clear fingerprints had elements of smudging.
3. Owners reported valuables, including jewellery stolen from the house and the safe under the dining room floor, but had been unwilling to itemise every item taken.
4. Third bedroom clearly used as office. Papers there relate to a business - I on U. Owners claim they've never heard of it. It's not their concern. The

> business belongs to a friend who uses the room as an office.

Hunter shook his head. The Morrisons had never come across his radar before, but he wanted to know more about them now.

CHAPTER THIRTY-TWO

HUNTER POURED HIMSELF ANOTHER COFFEE AND THEN TOOK HIS MUG on a walk to gather up the team in the incident room for a briefing. He didn't have much gathering to do as they were all there, except for Oskar Krol who wandered through from his own room.

He called the meeting to order. "First, the important business. How did the meal go for Gillian's birthday, Tim?"

"Fine thanks, boss." Tim grinned. "We had a good time. Could have done without John and Hector Hamilton poking their noses in, but apart from that, a good time was had by all."

"I'm glad to hear it. Yes, we let John and Hector out on bail. They were bound to insist on having a solicitor present, anyway. How did the interviews go Oskar?"

"It was all most interesting," said the DI. "Neil and I interviewed John first. He blamed the weed found in the flat on an unidentified friend of his brother's and claimed to know nothing about the cocaine in the sugar container. He now says his girlfriend is a croupier at a local casino and that he was embarrassed to say so."

"That's why he told us she worked as an estate agent, apparently," Neil said.

"Aye right," Colin said. "That man wouldn't know the truth if he saw a lie coming. He bit down into his apple viciously, as if it were John Hamilton's head.

"The man did admit that the small amount of cocaine in his desk was his," Oskar said.

"Only because he had no choice." Colin muttered.

"But his story about the ten thousand pounds was not the same as his brother's. Nor did he give us a straight answer to whether he had ever used a dating website," Neil said.

Hunter was standing nodding. "What did Hector say about the money?"

"That it was from the one client who went to get an accountant's certificate to prove it wasn't laundered cash," Oskar said.

"What's that got to do with the price of fish? It's not good enough for his legal obligations on money laundering," Hunter said.

"I know that you know that Hector knows that, but my feeling is it's the truth. The waffle we got from John about it coming from different clients and being partly petty cash seemed a bit of a stretch."

"What else did you learn?" Hunter asked.

"Hector was adamant that he doesn't do drugs and has asked John not to keep any in his flat. He seemed pretty exasperated when we told him about the weed and the cocaine." Oskar looked at Neil.

"Oskar put to him that John thought the weed might belong to a friend of his and he disputed that because he rarely brings anybody to the flat due to John and Katy's PDAs," Neil said.

"What's are PDAs when they're at home?" Hunter asked.

"Public displays of affection," the team chorused in reply.

"Yuck, imagine getting that close to John," Colin said.

Neil laughed. "I agree Colin, he's definitely not my type either. But boss, when we asked him about dating apps, he really took offence, didn't he Oskar?"

"He did. He said it was laughable that we should suggest that someone like him should need to use a dating app. But like John, he didn't actually deny it."

"That's interesting, because Eileen has told us she met her attacker through a dating website, hasn't she Rache?"

"Yes boss."

"Well, go on."

"Eileen's been quite consistent in what's she's told us. A colleague at work downloaded this new dating app onto her phone and she met the man calling himself Frederick through that. She tried to be careful by talking to him for a long time before she agreed to meet him."

"And when she did agree to meet him, it was in a public place. She really didn't do anything wrong, boss," Mel said.

"No, she didn't." Hunter agreed.

"But she did tell us that he looked a bit different when she met him to the photos she had seen online and on the facetime calls."

"Have we got those photos from the dating agency yet?" Oskar asked.

"No, client confidentiality, they claim." Nadia pulled a face as she said this.

"Them getting sued big time is closer to it, I'd bet," Bear said.

"I know her phone was missing when you found her, boss, but can the provider help with photos she may have kept on her phone?" Oskar asked.

"I doubt it. He was clever. Told her neither of them should keep photos of the other until they could get one together to keep forever." Rachael sighed. "He is such a bastard. Any move forward on focussing on the suspects?"

"Mansoor couldn't have done it himself. He was definitely inside at the time. It's too late for him to have been given any kind of day release or work pass," Nadia said.

"It doesn't mean he wasn't involved. He has a reach like an octopus," Tim said. "Did Meera get her reports to you today. boss?"

"Yes. I've just finished going through them. There seems to be no doubt that the two women who died after their attacks were murdered in the same way and therefore, by the same person. The way the assaults occurred, and the wounds inflicted were almost identical."

"What about Eileen Maguire?" Rachael asked.

"Eileen bravely agreed to allow Meera access to her hospital records if it would help find her attacker. And I hope it will. We can't let that young woman down. However, the attack was different. Possibly because the perpetrator is becoming more confident as he notches up successes."

"It doesn't bear thinking about, boss," Nadia said.

"I agree, Nadia. But rather than lure Eileen to a quiet place so he could attack her where there would be no witnesses, Eileen was invited for a fancy meal at a posh restaurant where there were lots of people who saw them."

"But none could accurately describe or identify him. People are notoriously unobservant," Tim said.

"True, young Myerscough, too true. But then, rather than take her outside to complete his attack in the quiet and the dark, he takes her through the restaurant when she is clearly in a drugged or intoxicated state and attacks her in the lift. It is different."

"The nurses told Rachael and I that the only way Eileen survived the shock and blood loss of her assault was because you and Meera found her so quickly, boss," Mel said.

"Yes, I heard that. The speed with which she got to the hospital was critical too. I did notice one thing that potentially links the cases. Meera's report on the first victim reveals that she had a match from the same dating website as Eileen and it was also with a man called Frederick."

"And that's the name Eileen's date used."

"Did he have a limp, boss?" Colin asked.

Hunter looked at Rachael. "Has Eileen said anything about a limp?"

"No boss. What's this about a limp, Colin?"

"Well, the boss will have noticed in our report that Nadia and I saw Eileen approach her date on the CCTV from the hotel bar near the restaurant. But we couldn't identify him because he always keeps his head down."

"I don't remember this," Hunter looked confused.

"Here's another copy if you want it."

"This was days ago. Why the fuck didn't you or Nadia flag it up sooner?"

"When nobody mentioned it, we thought you must consider it a dead end, boss."

"So, what in the name of God did this monster look like?" Bear asked.

"He was taller than average, maybe about the same height as the boss. Not like you or Tim," Nadia said. "It seemed like he had a thick, dark beard and dark hair. But he was clever, or lucky and never raised his head so we got a proper look at his face."

"But that's what I was getting at, he did have a limp. It's all in my report. Did nobody read it?" Colin sounded uncharacteristically exasperated.

"Have we got stills of the footage?" Hunter asked.

"That would be attached to the report, boss."

"Okay, Colin. Could you get me a copy of that report?"

"Nadia put it on your desk, boss."

"No, Colin. You put it on the desk. I filed a copy."

"Fuck," said Colin. "I filed it too." He blushed bright red, threw his apple core in the bin and went to retrieve a copy of the report.

"You're an idiot, sergeant and you're no better DC Chan." Hunter growled. "Oh, for fucks sake, what's done is done, Colin. By my rules we're all allowed one mistake. But this one counts for both you and Nadia."

Colin handed the report to Hunter. The acting DCI looked at the print from the CCTV, tore it from the report and stuck it on the white board. The picture showed the man with his head down and was taken from his right side. But it did reveal his height in relation to Eileen, his build, the top of his head, the shape of his profile and his beard.

"Shit this is a game changer," Mel said. "He's too slim to be John and too young to be Mr Morrison."

"Who's Mr. Morrison when he's at home?" Nadia asked.

"Jamie Thomson's next-door neighbour. His house was broken into, and the CSIs identified John's, Hector's, Felix's and Mansoor's prints at the scene. All of whom have been identified as potential assailants in this case," Tim said. "And Morrison says Mansoor is a family friend, and he was identified by some staff as a suspect."

"So was the boss. Are you sure the two cases are connected?"

"No, I'm not, Nadia, but it is strange there are so many echoes of the men identified in Eileen's case found to have been on the scene of that break-in."

"What's the connection between Mr Morrison and the men whose prints were found there?" Nadia asked.

"Jamie lives next door, John and Hector are his nephews and Mansoor is a family friend."

"He's deluded if he believes that. Mansoor is only a friend to himself." Bear said. "But where does Felix fit in? It doesn't sound like this Morrison fellow and Sir Felix Buchanan would move in the same social circles."

"Tim, you and Bear find out, will you? You know Felix as well as Lucky."

"We do boss, but I wouldn't say we're friendly."

"Makes no odds. Find out what's going on." Hunter frowned. "Now who is still in the frame, now we have this picture?"

"It can't be John, he's too fat," Mel said.

Hunter scored John Hamilton's name off the list.

"It's not Mansoor. He was in jail and the shape of the nose is wrong," Neil said.

"So that leaves us with Lucky, Felix and Hector, doesn't it? What about the limp? Did Eileen mention a limp?"

"No, boss. But I'll pop round to the hospital today and ask," Rachael said.

"Lucky complained that he hurt his foot when he was out running that evening and had to hitch a ride back to rehab," Tim said.

"And didn't Felix say he had twisted his ankle running for his flight home from Ibiza, Tim?" Hunter asked.

"He did, boss. They both had limps when we met with them."

"I noticed Hector has a limp," Oskar said. "It's slight. I suspect it's from an old injury or he was born with one leg slightly longer than the other."

"How can you know that Doctor DI?" Bear asked.

"I don't know, but I was a medical first responder in the Polish Army before I came here. It's a suggestion. I've seen many injuries and their results. I've also known enough people with leg length discrepancy to recognise the problems it can cause." Oskar paused. "He probably wears an orthotic lift in his shoe."

"Do we recall which leg they were favouring?" Hunter asked.

"I don't remember, boss. Do you?"

"Sadly not, Tim. If we'd seen this report earlier, I'd have paid more attention."

"Sorry, boss."

"It is what it is, Colin. We'll work with it now."

"Hector's left leg is shorter. He limps slightly to his left side," Oskar said.

Hunter wrote 'L' beside Hector's name.

"Okay, team. Today will be a busy day. Rachael, I want you meet with Eileen and see what she remembers. Tim, I want you and Bear go out to speak with Lucky and Felix. I really think I want them brought here for questioning. It's just more formal. But I don't want you two doing the interview here. Hand over to Colin and Nadia. No social contact there for them to play on."

"Yes boss."

"Oskar, you and Neil speak to John and Hector. We'll arrest John for possession of the drugs now. He'll still stay out on bail, but there's nothing we can do about that. I want you to question Hector more about the money found in the office and his connection with Morrison. Pin him down on why his prints were found on the underfloor safe. The CSIs found traces of liquid inside the safe."

"Mel, you and I will go around to the Morrisons. Ask about that liquid and tell him whose prints we've found. To be honest, if Mansoor's involved, his agent will be a professional and would have worn gloves. Find out more about that relationship."

"Will do boss."

"Colin, you and Nadia get back to the hotel with photos of our three main suspects. See if you can jog any memories." Hunter looked around the room.

"I thought we were to interview Lucky and Felix."

"True, but it'll take Tim and Bear a lot longer to get to and from the estate than for you to get to and from a city centre hotel."

"Don't count on it, boss," Nadia said.

"No smart-arse remarks, DC Chan. And remember, I want every report on my desk. Don't fucking file them."

CHAPTER
THIRTY-THREE

Tim led Lucky and Felix into the station. Bear followed them in, and they were shown to interview rooms one and two respectively. Lucky looked around the small, dark room and noticed the only window had bars across it and was high up the wall. There was no way he was going to see out of it. The bars were covered by disgusting, thick cobwebs. Lucky held his nose. He had forgotten just how nasty these rooms were and the smell was not at all fresh. Maybe a coffee would mask the smell. He asked Tim if that would be possible. Tim nodded and held the door open for the young PC who would guard it and then left to fetch the drink.

When Tim returned, Lucky said, "What are we going to talk about today? Bloody hell, Tim. This coffee's out of a machine. What are you thinking about? Get us a decent one."

"Sorry, Lucky, we won't be chatting. My colleagues will be along in a few minutes. As for the coffee, that's it, I'm afraid."

Lucky watched as Tim left the room and failed to get any response from the PC either.

. . .

In the room next door, Felix sat on the metal chair on the far side of the table that Bear had indicated. He looked around. He was horrified by how musty the room was and the tables and chairs were bolted to the floor. The recording device on the table was bolted on to it too and high on the wall was a camera. He looked up at it and smiled, wondering if anybody was watching him at that moment.

There was a policewoman by the door. Felix looked at her and winked. She was pretty but made no reaction. He wriggled around on his seat to look at the wall behind him. The peeling paint was ugly, and the movement hurt his ankle. His reward was to locate the only window, but it was too high up for him to see anything even if the cobwebs had not obscured it. The pain hadn't been worth it. This place smelt bad too. How could anybody work in this environment, especially somebody like Tim who did it voluntarily?

He was brought back to the present by Bear's offer of a coffee, but when Felix discovered it was from a machine he declined. This room was bad enough without adding cheap coffee to the mix.

Colin and Nadia decided to interview Lucky first. Before they went into the interview room they whispered together.

"Good cop/bad cop," Nadia said.

"Of course. Which one do you fancy today?"

"How about I do bad cop now and you play that role when we interview Felix?"

Colin nodded and they entered the room.

"Lord Buchanan, thank you for your help with our enquiries," Colin said. He turned on the tape and introduced those in the room. He explained that the interview would be recorded on tape and film.

"I don't think I have to be here, but the big men didn't make it sound like an invitation." Lucky retorted. "I'm not under arrest, am I?"

"No. Should you be?" Nadia asked.

"Not at all. I'm just checking because that means I can leave at any time."

"Indeed, you can, Lord Buchanan."

"But we might draw an inference that you had something to hide if you did." Nadia added.

"She doesn't let much go, does she?" Lucky nodded at Colin.

"Nothing at all." Nadia replied.

"Now, can we discuss the night of Eileen Maguire's attack?" Colin asked. "You were still and in-patient at the Darling Rehabilitation Centre and coming towards the end of your treatment."

"Correct."

"A member of staff informed one of our colleagues that you completed the course very well. A model patient."

"That's good to hear. I tried." Lucky's expression was serious, and he looked down at his hands as he replied.

"She also explained that patients are permitted outside of the grounds as they near the end of their stay. Was that element of trust afforded to you?"

"Yes, it was. But it's hard. The dealers know about it and wait in the road at the end of the drive. They offer uppers, downers, coke, hash, heroine, anything you might want and staying clean isn't made easy by that."

"Were you tempted?" Nadia asked.

"Absolutely. I nearly cracked the first time it happened."

"What did you do?"

"I ran back up the drive to my room and locked the door until the cravings receded."

"Commendable. So did you not go out after that?"

"I did. You really must, so they know you can cope in the real world. I tended to leave early in the morning, because the dealers and junkies aren't known for being early risers, or later at night after dinner when they had left for the day."

"What did you do when you were out?" Colin asked.

"I've always loved riding and there was a stable down the road. I enjoyed going out on the horses. They don't judge. I even enjoyed mucking out. It reminded me of the smells and sensations I experienced as a young boy."

"What else did you do?"

"I used to go for coffee in one of the local cafes. I usually tried to go to the one with the prettiest waitresses."

"Anything else?" Nadia asked.

"I'd go for a pint in the pub."

"Were you ever offered drugs there?"

"Once. But the landlord threw the dealer out. Said he wasn't having any muck in his pub. That made it easy for me." Lucky paused and looked up at the tape recorder. "Not much has been easy for me since my father died."

"Forgive me if I don't sympathise with the titled Earl whose grand home and estate cover so much of the Lothians." Nadia sneered. "So apart for riding, ogling the local girls and downing pints in the local, what else did you find to do with your newfound freedom?"

"I started looking after myself again. For a time I didn't

care, but I shower every day, keep my hair and beard neat and I've been going to the gym and running. I find that running allows my mind to be free and forget about the bad stuff. I'm training for a marathon next month and hope to do the London Marathon this year."

"Long distance running. Are you any good?" Nadia asked.

"I keep going but I'm not fast."

"The records show that you went out running on the evening of the day Eileen Maguire was attacked. Where did you go? What route did you take?"

"That's the girl who was attacked in the Waldorf Astoria. I was in a rehab centre in East Lothian. I didn't run that far."

"How far did you run before you hitched a lift?" Nadia asked.

"I ran all the way. I only had to hitch a lift on the way home. I hurt my ankle. It's one of the perils of running in the dark."

"Who gave you the lift?"

"John his name was. Looked like a banker or an accountant. Suit and tie and so on."

"What route did you take that night?"

"I can't remember exactly, but I tried to keep off the major roads. That's why it took me so long to hitch a lift."

"What were you wearing?"

"I didn't go to dinner in my running gear, if that's what you think."

"What did you wear to dinner?" Nadia asked. "The room at the Waldorf Astoria was booked under an assumed name and secured with a cash payment. Did you regularly go into the city during your practice runs?"

"It was against the rules to leave the area. I wasn't in the city."

"Which ankle did you hurt, Lord Buchanan?" Colin asked.

"My left ankle. Now, if that's all, I need a cigarette and a decent coffee. This muck is revolting."

"Something we can all agree on. Thank you for your time. If you wait in reception, somebody will take you and your cousin back your home after we've interviewed him." Colin shook hands with Lucky and Nadia led him back to reception.

"Do you believe him, Nadia?"

"Not all of it. I doubt breaking the rules upsets his lordship as much as he would have us think it does. But I don't think he attacked Eileen."

"Neither do I. And I don't think he'd have been far enough through his programme to be permitted off the grounds when the first two women were murdered."

"Agreed. He's an arse, but not a murderer."

Felix was angry at being kept waiting in this smelly little room for so long. Especially when the PC at the door wouldn't even chat. When Colin and Nadia walked in, he asked for a bottle of water and a bag of cheese and onion crisps. He was pleased when the PC was dispatched to fetch the order.

While they were waiting, for the PC to return, Nadia explained to Felix that he was there voluntarily to help them with their enquiries. He was not under arrest and was free to leave at any time. She watched Felix stand up and smiled as Colin spoke.

"Of course, if you were unwilling to assist us and left without doing so, that might change our view of you and your importance to the case."

Felix sat down. He scowled. "What case are we talking about? It's not that misunderstanding in Ibiza is it. The police never did serve their warrant. At least I've not seen it."

"We may chat about that, but no." Colin turned when he heard the PC come back into the room. She deposited the water and crisps onto the table and resumed her place at the door. Colin said that the interview would be recorded orally and visually and introduced all the people in the room.

"Now," Nadia began. "Sir Felix, you are here to assist us about the attack that occurred in the Waldorf Astoria Hotel. Have you ever been there, or dined at The Pompadour Restaurant?"

"I've never stayed at the hotel, but I've been there often enough, weddings, business meetings, social events. You know the kind of thing. And I adore The Pompadour. The food is exquisite and the service outstanding. I highly recommend it."

"When did you last visit The Pompadour?" Nadia asked.

"Too long ago."

"Could you be more specific?"

"A couple of months maybe. I like it best when someone else is paying and with Lucky being in rehab recently, he's not been about to share the load. You know the kind of thing."

"I'm not sure that I do," Nadia said. "Were you there the evening Eileen Maguire was attacked?"

"Not at all. I heard about it. One reads about these kinds of things in the paper and so on, but no, I wasn't there that night. Apparently one of the lifts was out of use for hours. That must have been irritating for the guests."

"Worse for the woman who was attacked, I suspect." Nadia breathed in deeply. This guy was unreal. She was desperately trying to control herself sufficiently so that she didn't sound unprofessional. But he was the living end. "Where were you then, that night?"

"I can't quite remember. Probably playing a gig. I do a lot of DJing, you know. Getting to be quite the international traveller for that."

"I'm not sure one gig in Ibiza qualifies for such extravagant claims. But if you don't know where you were, how can you be so sure that you weren't at the Waldorf Astoria?"

"Because I hadn't been there for such a long time. If you gave me my phone, I could check my calendar."

"Don't worry we'll check."

"Where did you stay when Lord Buchanan was in rehab?" Colin asked.

"Just at his estate. He needed me to oversee things for him."

"Did he pay you a fee for that service?"

"Why? A small retainer, I suppose. Just to keep things above board, you know the kind of thing."

"The reason I ask is that you mentioned that you prefer to go for expensive meals when someone else is paying," Colin said. "I just wondered if you had any financial problems we should know about."

"Not at all. Not at all."

"It's just that when we checked your bank accounts it seemed Lucky was paying you two thousand pounds a week, for precious little work. Why would he do that?" Nadia asked.

"As I say, to keep himself right with the accountants."

"Hmm." Nadia looked across at him. "Sir Felix, you had much larger sums going out to an account that we have traced to the name of Arjun Mansoor. It took you over your overdraft limit on several occasions and the funds from Lucky just pulled you back."

"How do you know Mr. Mansoor?" Colin asked. "He is certainly not genteel company and he's almost always bad news."

"Unless we must, I'd rather not discuss Mr. Mansoor. Can I get out for a ciggie? We've been here ages."

"No reason why not. DC Chan will accompany you. There's no smoking in the building but she can go with you to the car park."

When the interview reconvened, Colin started by asking Felix about his gig in Ibiza. "Why did you initially say you had been there just under a week? We've found out that you were there less than twenty-four hours."

"Well, that's less than a week."

"Come on, Felix."

"That's Sir Felix to you."

"Really? Fine. Sir Felix, the Spanish police have told us that you left the island almost immediately after your gig to avoid being questioned about an attack on a young woman who attended the event."

"Nonsense, it was all a misunderstanding. She gave me the nod and then backed off. Little tart."

"But you didn't tell us any of this," Colin said.

"Well, it's not relevant, is it? Nothing came of it."

"Sir Felix, can't you see that an accusation of violence against a young woman is extremely relevant when we are investigating a similar attack?" Nadia almost growled her question.

"No. The Spanish girl was talking bollocks and I wasn't at the Waldorf Astoria. None of it is relevant and none of it is your business."

"Let's move on," Colin said. "A house was broken into on West Mains Road a night or two ago. Your fingerprints were found at the scene. Can you tell us how they got there, please?"

"Where was this?" Felix asked. He blushed a deep red to the roots of his hair.

"A semi-detached house in West Mains Road."

"Gosh not really my kind of place I'm afraid. There must be some mistake."

"I don't doubt it, and you made it when you left your prints." Nadia paused, then looked at Colin before she continued to speak. "I think it has something to do with Arjun Mansoor and the reason why you didn't want to talk about him. How close to the truth am I?"

"Too close. I suppose I might as well tell you because Arjun will daub me in it anyway."

"True."

"He pretty much runs the drug supply in Edinburgh now. Has done for a while."

"Carry on, Sir Felix."

"I got a bit behind on my payments to him. I take a couple of lines of coke to jolly myself up when I'm running a gig." He looked at the detectives' expressionless faces and took a deep breath before he continued. "He told me I could work it off by selling to punters at gigs."

"Be careful, Sir Felix, you have just admitted to supplying a class A drug. Do you want a lawyer?"

"I suppose it might be best."

"I think it would."

"Could I have another bottle of water and time out for a fag too?"

"Yes, we'll arrange that," Colin said. "We'll have to hold you in the cells until your brief gets here. Do you want a sandwich or something?"

"Yes, please."

Colin suspended the interview and asked the PC to take Sir Felix to the cells. "Will you arrange for someone to take Lucky home, Nadia. There's going to be a long wait and we might as well get him home. By the way Sir Felix, which ankle did you twist running for your flight home from Ibiza?"

"My right ankle. Bloody sore it was too."

Hunter was surprised to see Colin and Nadia wander into the incident room. He followed them in and asked how their interviews with Lucky and Felix had gone.

"Lucky is an arse, but probably not a murderer, boss. The distance and timing just don't add up," Colin said.

"And he couldn't go running in clothes suitable to dine at the Pompadour, neither would he gain entrance to the dining room in the evening dressed in running gear. It doesn't add up." Nadia added. "He is an unpleasant man, but not our murderer, I don't think. Colin, would you like a tea or coffee?"

"No, I've got a bottle of water here. I think I'll take this break as time for lunch."

"What's Maggie made you today?"

"Never mind what's in the bloody sandwiches. How did the interview with Felix go?"

"We've had to suspend it, boss. He's asked for a brief. In fact, I suggested he get a lawyer. He all but confessed to dealing drugs as an agent for Arjun Mansoor."

"Perfectly possible, Colin. That man has form."

"Yes, but I didn't want him to spill his guts without having the opportunity of legal advice."

"I'd have let him daub himself in it. Weasel of a man, he is," Bear said. "If you're making yourself a tea, Nadia, could I get a coffee?"

"And what did your last slave die of?"

"Hard work." Bear grinned.

Nadia shook her head. "You are too predictable, Bear." She laughed and spooned the brown grit into his mug.

"I think you and Nadia have done the right thing, Colin."

"I got a uniform to take Lucky back to the estate and another is getting Felix a sandwich. I think this could go on for a while."

"Did Felix say how he and Mansoor are connected?"

"Drugs and money. Mansoor's usual interests."

"Okay, keep me posted. Has anybody seen Oskar?"

"Here Hunter. How may I help?"

"Come through. Let's have a chat. And Tim and Bear, I'd like you to go through all the statements for this murder case and the attack on Eileen. I want you to work out which of our suspects could have possibly committed all three crimes."

"But we don't know exactly when the murders were committed, boss. We just know when the bodies were found," Tim said.

"No, but the post-mortem reports will give you a best guess as to date of death."

"Nadia, that's Felix's brief here. Charlie just phoned from reception."

"Okay, Colin. Let me finish my tea and we'll go down."

When Colin and Nadia walked into the interview room, they immediately recognised the lawyer. It was the same woman who had been into HMP Edinburgh the day they went to interview Mansoor.

She stood up as they walked towards her and shook hands. "Della Maclehose," she said. "You must be DS Reid and DC Chan."

The woman was taller than Colin remembered.

"Have you had time to take instructions from your client, Ms Maclehose?" Colin asked.

"Indeed, I have, and Sir Felix will not be answering any further questions, but he has asked me to read a prepared statement. Shall I proceed?"

"Go ahead," Nadia said. She sat back on her chair and stared at Felix throughout.

"I, Sir Felix Buchanan, residing at the Buchanan family estate with my cousin, Lord Lachlan Buchanan, was not present at the Pompadour Restaurant, nor any other part of the Waldorf Astoria Hotel, the night Eileen Maguire was attacked. I was not involved in that assault.

"I have had financial problems that result from my addiction to cocaine and use of marijuana supplied to me by agents of Arjun Mansoor. My debt was allowed to grow and then suddenly the whole balance was demanded, failing which, I was informed I would be required to pay double the amount outstanding, which I did not have. The alternatives offered to me were threats of grievous bodily

harm or carrying out favours for Mr Mansoor's associates. I chose to carry out the favours because I did not want to be regularly assaulted.

"The favours demanded of me were to carry cocaine to gigs at which I was DJing because I would not be searched and give them to Mansoor's dealers in return for envelopes of cash. I gained no financial advantage from these transactions and was required to give the envelopes to Mr. Mansoor's associates, unopened.

"One of these associates was Mr Morrison of West Mains Road. I arrived at his house where I was required to deliver the envelopes from gigs. When I got there, I found the front door was opened and I went in. I shouted to make my presence known, but there was no reply. The house was empty.

"Lots of things had been trashed and the carpet in the dining room was slashed. I looked at the hole and found a black box beside a safe under the floorboards. The safe had been broken and any other contents removed. The floor was wet, but I do not know what had been spilt. I heard the owners coming in and cursing at the open door. I fled out of the back door, jumped over the back garden wall and ran away because I did not want to be blamed for a burglary that I didn't commit.

"I have since taken the envelopes to Mr Morrison. He was very angry with me because he received them later than he expected. I know nothing more about the attack on Ms Maguire or the break-in at the Morrison's home."

Della Maclehose looked up from her notebook. "My client is willing to sign this statement, after which, I suggest arrangements be made to take him home. Don't you agree, detectives?"

"Sign it," Colin said. "Then, Ms Maclehose, we'll charge

your client with supply of class A drugs, namely cocaine, release him on bail and get him home. But Felix."

"Sir Felix," Della said.

"Sir Felix, if we subsequently find you have omitted anything, I will throw the book at you. Do you understand?"

Della looked at her client. Colin noticed that he stared straight at her when he agreed to his terms.

"Fine. Let's wrap this up."

CHAPTER
THIRTY-FOUR

JAMIE WAS AWOKEN, NOT BY THE USUAL SQUEALS AND GIGGLES COMING from the twins' bedroom. Nor by Princess Leia licking his face, but by a hammer working a 'For Sale' sign into the front garden of the house next door. Great, he thought. He told Linda about the development and that he planned to get their bid in today. Then he looked at the board. Who the hell gets an estate agent in North Berwick for a house in the middle of Edinburgh? Not his problem. It wouldn't make any difference to the success of his offer.

Linda got up. "Jamie I'm off for a shower. I want to be ready for Eileen because today is the day Eileen will meet the guide dog that had been assigned to her. I'm worried."

"Why?"

"Eileen had always preferred cats and I can't help wondering how she, or her daft cat, Princess Leia, will take to a dog in the mix. I'm also wondering how Eileen got to the top of the guide dog list so fast. I know so many people are waiting for a dog."

"I might know something about that, but it's not my secret to tell. You enjoy your shower and I'm going to phone Pop."

The phone rang out. Bugger, Pop must have a new number. Jamie didn't stop to think that his pop shouldn't have a phone at all. He was irritated that he couldn't get hold of Ian immediately. He'd have to wait until his pop phoned him. It wouldn't be long. He knew that.

He dressed quickly and went down to the kitchen and put the kettle on. Jamie wandered into the glass porch at the front of the house and watched the estate agent as he took photos and then rang the doorbell. He was surprised when Mrs Morrison opened the door and kissed the man. A bit forward, Jamie thought.

He heard the kettle finish boiling and went to make his cuppa. Then he took his brew back to the porch. The estate agent reversed a black van into the driveway. Jamie saw him glance in his direction and frown. Then his phone rang. It was an unknown number. Pop.

"New phone?" Jamie asked.

"Hello Pop. How are you would have been nice, lad."

"Aye. Probably. Look, Pop, the Morrison's is up for sale."

"Text me the name and number of the agents."

"Pop, there's something odd happening. I'll send that to you, but I've got to go. I'm window hinging."

Jamie hung up but sent the text his Pop needed. What was going on? The estate agent was moving a whole lot of stuff from the house. Why? What? He saw glass bottles, but he couldn't make out the contents. Then the boxes. What was in the boxes? What was that? Flasks? What the hell. The estate agent continued to move things out of the house and into the back of the van. He kissed Mrs Morrison on the cheek and shook Mr Morrison's hand as they closed up the van together.

It was then Mr Morrison patted the back door of the van and Jamie watched his face. He read his lips as Morrison said Mansoor. Then the homeowner also jumped into the van.

Fucking Arjun Mansoor. Jamie couldn't let that sit. He dumped his mug on the porch table.

"Just out for a bit, Linda."

"A bit of what? I thought you were working at the showroom today."

"Gotta go, love. Tell Frankie I'll be in later."

"Jamie, wait!"

Jamie didn't wait. He jumped into his car and pulled out of the driveway. He ended up two cars behind the black van at the lights. This would do. This would do nicely. He drove along West Mains Road until it became Blackford Avenue. He was fine. Much less likely to be spotted with two cars between them. Where was it going? The first car turned off onto Observatory Road. Still one car between them, then an old blue Mondeo jumped the lights at West Saville Terrace and Jamie was back to being two cars behind. His phone rang, Pop. He couldn't stop to take the call now.

He had forgotten what a long street Blackford Avenue was. Blast. The first car continued on while he had to veer onto Oswald Road. Still, at least the Mondeo was still there.

Jamie looked around. The Grange was a lovely part of the city. Maybe he should stop by soon and do a bit of night visiting. He was sure there would be plenty of goodies for the taking behind the doors of the traditional Victorian homes here. He hadn't been out for a while. Mind you, he might be a bit busy helping Linda with Eileen. Maybe he'd put thieving on the back burner.

Bugger. Where was the Mondeo going? It had turned off onto Blackford Road. What street was Jamie on? It kept changing names. Kilgraston Road now. His phone rang again. Pop. He still couldn't do anything about it now. The last thing he wanted was to be stopped for driving while he was on the phone and not be able to follow the van. At last, he turned from Marchmont Road onto Melville Drive. The van driver seemed to have spotted him, he sped up, but there were too many traffic lights and buses to go fast for long.

Through the Meadows and onto Gillespie Place. Jamie had no doubt that the van would turn off at Gillespie Crescent where Mansoor's wife and son still lived in his ground floor apartment. Jamie watched the van signal to turn exactly as he had expected. No way he was going in there. It was a dead end and there was never any place to park. He drove on towards Bruntsfield and would drive to the showroom. His phone rang again. Linda. He couldn't take her call either because he was driving. He knew he'd get grief later.

When Jamie got to the showroom, Donna was making coffee while Frankie chatted to a punter who clearly didn't have two beans to rub together. Maybe they could get rid of that old green Renault that had been sitting there forever and had done more miles than Lewis Hamilton. Jamie would be glad to get rid of that one. He took the keys to Frankie.

"I have a couple of calls to make, Frankie, but maybe the gentleman would like to see the nice green car that just came in? It's not been valeted yet (it was valeted so long ago it was again covered in muck and dust) and don't discount it (give it away if you have to)."

Jamie knew Frankie could read between the lines.

"I thought you were saving that one for the wee blonde lassie," Frankie said.

"I think the engine is too big for her to handle." Jamie grinned at the potential purchaser and walked to the office to make the calls.

Pop first.

"Where the fuck have you been. I've called you twice, you wee bastard."

"Well, you would know, Pop. There was something funny going on at the Morrisons so I followed the estate agents' van. Mr Morrison went with him."

"Where to?"

"They emptied a whole lot of containers and boxes from the house and took it Mansoor's flat."

"What like?"

"I don't know, do I? I can't see through metal or cardboard and even the glass containers, I couldn't make out what was in them."

"Don't give up your day job or apply to be 007, will you? So could you see any more when they unloaded it?"

"No, they turned into Gillespie Crescent. I just kept going on the main road and came here. I thought I might call Blondie and get him to take a look."

"Aye, that'll work. Oh, and by the way, you've bought a house."

"That's grand Pop. I'll tell Linda."

Jamie hung up and called Linda. "We've got the house. There'll be a room for Eileen if she wants to stay."

"Good. That's good. I'll tell her. And what was all that about this morning?"

"I'll tell you, but not over the phone. See you tonight, Linda."

"But Eileen's meeting her guide dog today. Aren't you coming up to the hospital?"

"Can't do that babe. Too much going on. I expect I'll see enough of it soon." Jamie heard a click and realised Linda had hung up on him. It couldn't be helped. He had things to do.

He dialled Tim's number and was confused when Mel answered the call.

"Jamie, hello."

"Mel? I thought I'd dialled Blondie, but I suppose you'll do."

"Thanks, you sweet talking Casanova. Tim's hands are covered in mayonnaise, so when I saw it was you calling, I picked up his phone."

"Look what you and Blondie get up to in the privacy of the police station is none of my business. But there is something I need to tell you."

Mel ended the call to Jamie and ran along the corridor to Hunter's room. She knocked once and opened the door. She could see Hunter was pouring over the statements relating to Eileen's case.

"Mel, this seems urgent. I could do with a break. Want a coffee?"

"No thanks, boss, it's a bit too strong for me, but I've just come off the phone to Jamie Thomson. I think you'll want to hear what he had to say."

She watched as Hunter poured himself a mug of the strong, black coffee. "Make this good news, Mel. A breakthrough would be best." Hunter sat down again to listen to what she had to say.

"Oskar, come through, will you?" Hunter said "Mel has some news about the Morrisons' house next-door to Jamie Thomson and a possible link to Arjun Mansoor. I want you to get a warrant to search both that house and Mansoor's flat on the basis that there may be drugs, drug money or drug paraphernalia on the premises."

Hunter stared at Oskar. He didn't move.

"Go on, chop chop," Hunter said.

"On what grounds do we suspect this?"

"Did you and Mel discover anything when you spoke to Mr. Morrison?"

"Nothing useful. And this stuff was being specifically removed from the house at West Mains Road to Mansoor's flat in Gillespie Crescent before the viewings for the house sale began?"

"Mel, go with Oskar to his room and tell him what you told me while he's drafting the request. I want you two to interview the Morrisons again while their place is being taken apart. And send Tim through, will you? I want him to go to the showroom and have a chat with Jamie."

"Yep, boss. Come on inspector, come with me and all shall be revealed."

"I'll look forward to that." Oskar smiled.

. . .

"Blondie, what can I do for you?" Jamie called out to Tim across the showroom. "I was looking for you earlier, but Mel answered your phone and told me you and she were rolling in mayonnaise or chocolate sauce or something. I got quite hard thinking about it."

"That should be DC Grant to you, and sorry to disappoint you Jamie. I was only eating a burger. But I believe you saw something that might be of use to us. Why did the likes of you phone it in?"

"The likes of me, DC Myerscough. That's not very nice." Jamie looked up at Tim. "But I thought it might cause difficulties for Pop's auld enemy, Mansoor. So, I suppose I felt obliged. Coffee?"

"Go on then, I will. And you can tell me what you saw the Morrison's and their estate agent getting up to."

"I will, once you've explained how Eileen got to the top of the guide dog priority list in one jump after an anonymous million-pound donation to the charity."

"Aah, well. I might not give you all the details."

"That's what I thought. Thanks Tim. For a cop, you're a decent man."

"Thanks, I think."

"Sit down. I'll tell you all I know."

"I don't really like dogs very much," Linda could hear the panic in Eileen's voice from the other end of the corridor.

"I think you might like this one, Eileen. His name's Rory."

"That's a silly name for a dog."

"Says my sister whose cat is called Princess Leia. Really Eileen, don't go looking for problems," Linda said.

"Thanks for the support," Eileen said. "I'm just not used to dogs."

"I know, but this boy is extremely handsome, Eileen. And he's so well behaved. Look at him."

"He's here because I can't, you idiot, Linda."

Noah, the man from the guide dog association, spoke softly. "We chose Rory for you because we know you haven't ever had a dog before and this boy is very gentle. He has a sweet spot where he loves getting tickled, right behind his ear. Give me your hand and I'll show you where he likes to be touched."

Linda reached out her hand and the man helped her to stroke Rory's head.

"He has a beautiful coat; it feels so silky." Eileen said.

"He does, don't you Rory? And we'll teach you how to look after him and keep it that way." The man stretched Eileen's hand a little further forward. "And there's that sweet spot I was telling you about."

"I can feel him pushing his head into my hand. Which ear is it?"

"Either and both. He likes to be made a fuss of. Here, why don't you give him a dog treat. You'll be his friend for life after that." The man put the small, round thing into Eileen's hand.

"How do I do it?"

"Just reach out and open your hand. He'll do the rest."

Eileen felt the dog's soft mouth take the treat from the palm of her hand.

"Well done, Eileen," the man said.

"Can I stroke him?" Linda asked.

"Not right now. I want him to concentrate on Eileen."

"Of course. Silly of me. He is lovely, sis. And I think he could help you get around."

"This is just a first meeting. If you like him well enough, I'll bring him back tomorrow. Would you like that?"

"Yes, yes please. I think I would. Does he like cats?"

"He'll live very happily with your cat, Eileen. You and Rory need to get to know each other and learn to work together. It'll take a while for you to get used to each other, but we'll help you and be with you every step of the way."

"I'll put the work in. I must. I have no choice. Frederick made sure of that."

"Linda, will you stay with me? That lawyer Jamie's pop knows, Mr, Donovan is coming to see me and talk about compensation, but I don't want to meet him alone."

"I'll stay. I thought we might go down to the cafeteria for a coffee, too."

"I'd like that. Just a change of air and to get out of the ward. Thanks sis. Bye, then Rory. Pat you tomorrow," Eileen said.

I've never had a cat, but there have always been dogs in the family, so I am used to them. We tend to go for big dogs, labradors, setters and springer spaniels. That type of breed.

Eileen told me she's more of a cat person than a dog person. I can't help wondering how she'll get on with a guide dog. Time will tell. I watch her progress, but only from a distance, just in case she works out I'm me, by sound or smell.

It would have been easier for me if she'd died. She's getting so much attention and pity. You know the kind of thing.

CHAPTER THIRTY-FIVE

"YOU LOOK BEAUTIFUL, GILLIAN," TIM SAID.

"Thank you. I like that new shirt is it Gucci?"

"It is. You're getting better at spotting different designers."

"And I can spot a fake at ten paces, now. But why is Ailsa treating us to a meal when it's her birthday?"

"Today she turns thirty and inherits personal control of the funds our mother left in trust for her."

"Gosh, then will she be as wealthy as you are?"

"A little more so. I just gave one million pounds to Guide Dogs for the Blind, remember?"

"I don't see why you had to do that. Eileen Maguire is not your responsibility."

"Maybe not. But I was able to make her life easier, secure the charity's future for years to come, and I won't notice the difference in my bank balance."

"Yet you work as a detective constable and won't even take advantage of the fast-track scheme available to graduates. You're a funny one, Timothy Myerscough." She kissed him on the lips, applied a little perfume to her pulse points and picked up her mulberry handbag. "I'm ready to go when you are."

"Come on, the taxi will be here anytime. Let's see if Ailsa's ready."

"Is Kenneth not driving us in?"

"No, Ailsa has another guest. Kenneth is driving them, I think."

"Is this the man in her life that she's been so secretive about?"

"I hope so. I want to meet him."

When they arrived at the Waldorf Astoria, Simon Land was already waiting in the foyer. Tim watched as he approached Ailsa and complimented her on her dress and her hair. The man kissed her gently, touched her blonde curls and Ailsa smiled.

Simon turned to Tim and Gillian. He shook Tim by the hand and double air-kissed Gillian.

"Believe me, Tim, when I say that your sister refused to let me treat her for her birthday dinner. Apparently, she has a surprise and she wanted to host."

"She hasn't told you?"

"Told me what?"

"Well, I don't want to steal her thunder. Let's go through."

Tim guided the group to follow Ailsa into the dining room. A bottle of Dom Perignon was chilling on ice at their table and Tim was happy to see his sister looking so happy.

When the waiter arrived, Ailsa specified that her guests should have guest menus. Tim saw Gillian's quizzical expression.

"No prices." He whispered.

When they had ordered, Ailsa took a deep breath, but before she could speak, Lucky and Felix walked in and came over to their table.

"DP, how delightful. May we join you, Timmy?" Felix asked.

"This is my table, not Tim's. He is my guest and no, you may not join us,"

"Dr Myerscough, how unkind. Shall we just have a glass of fizz and raise a toast with you."

"You will not."

Gillian stood up. "I don't know who you are, but please leave us alone to enjoy our evening." She stared at Felix.

"My goodness, what beautiful green eyes. Lucky, have you seen these? Is this Tim's girlfriend you told me about? I've never seen such a distinct green hue and the flash in the hair does it justice." He touched Gillian's hair. She smacked his hand. Tim stood up.

"Don't ruin my sister's birthday meal, Felix. I think that gentleman is waiting to show you to your table."

"Indeed. And if I recall, you are familiar with the menu, sir."

"Of course. Always good to cross paths with friends. Sir Felix Buchanan, at your service any time, darling." He kissed Gillian's hand and followed Lucky to their table.

Tim was pleased to see it was at the other side of the restaurant.

"You do know some creepy people, Tim. Scum like that make me pleased to be going to Moscow, where I'll be treated with respect." Gillian said.

Felix turned back. "You're leaving the country?"

"Yes. In a couple of days. Not that it's any of your business," Gillian said.

"Never mind him," Tim said. "What were you going to tell us, Ailsa?"

Ailsa announced to the table that she now had full responsibility for her trust fund account and that she had taken advice from her accountant and planned to make a business investment.

"I would like to invest five hundred thousand pounds of capital into Land's Farm to allow Simon and Robin to create an area to teach children where their food comes from. A children's farm, if you like."

Simon looked at her. "What? Ailsa, no, pet. I can't accept."

"It's not a gift, it's an investment. I want legal documentation drawn up."

"But your proposal won't cost Robin and I nearly that amount to put together."

"That's fine. Keep the rest as cash in the bank for work needing done to improve the farm as it needs. I think it's important that city children know about animals and crops and the sustainability of our planet. I am donating a similar amount to the city farm to secure its future." She looked at Simon. "I won't take no for an answer, so you might as well accept gracefully."

"Wait til I tell Robin that he's in charge of the development of the children's farm. He'll be delighted. Cheers, darling. Thank you. We won't let you down."

"I know, I won't let you."

CHAPTER THIRTY-SIX

Oskar and Mel led Mr and Mrs Morrison into the station.

"We appreciate your time today," Oskar said.

"You mean you want us out of the way while you search our home," Mrs Morrison said.

"It won't be ours for much longer. We're moving back to East Lothian to be nearer the family. That wee tyke next door bought it for a song, but he's such a brat we just wanted rid of it." Mr Morrison frowned and looked at Oskar. "Well, let's get this over with, Inspector."

They went into the same cramped interview room that Hector had been in before.

"I know a good decorator. Looks like you need one." Mr Morrison sat on the chair at the far side of the table with a familiarity that made Mel think he had done this before. "Why do you still bolt on those old recording machines? There are much more modern ones available."

Oskar explained that Mr Morrison and his wife were helping with enquiries and not under arrest. They were not under any obligation to stay but their assistance was appreciated. He stated that the interview would be recorded visually and audibly and introduced those in the room for the benefit of the tape.

Oskar was interested by Mr Morrison. Although he was in his late forties, he remained in better shape than most of his contemporaries and still worked as an optician for Vision-Savers a chain of opticians well known in the city.

"When did you decide to become an optician, Mr Morrison?" Mel asked.

"When I did rubbish in my Highers and couldn't be a doctor. You'd be surprised how many opticians, nurses and pharmacists are the same."

"Rather different careers to make such a generalised statement, I would think."

"No. A bit like you became a copper when you failed the physical to be a fire officer."

"I never wanted to be a fire officer, thank you," Mel said. Then she bit her lip as she saw that Morrison had got the rise out of her that he wanted.

"I'm new to the city," Oskar said. "I understand you count a Mr Arjun Mansoor amongst your family friends. How did you meet Mr Mansoor?"

"He was one of my patients and took an interest in all the tests I had to perform. We often discussed eyes, sight, and blindness."

"But it became more than that?"

"Yes. He knows my nephew, John and became a family friend when we discovered the connection."

"He has been in jail several years now and you visit him more often than his wife does. Isn't that a little strange?"

"I help him keep his business running. Sometimes my

visits are business related. Other times, social. I don't know about his wife."

"Would that be his drug dealing business you assist with?" Oskar asked.

"Good grief, I don't think so."

"But you know that's what he's in jail for?" Mel asked.

"Look, dear, I just collect funds from his associates, count their takings, and then get the money to his wife and she banks it. I'm doing my best for a friend fallen on hard times. That's all."

"Did Mansoor ever express an interest in different colours of eyes?"

"Oh yes, and how that occurred. He's an intelligent man with an enquiring mind. Most interesting company."

Mrs Morrison confirmed all her husband had said but stated that she had never met Mr Mansoor and expressed irritation that he used their third bedroom to keep the financial records for his business.

"I think we'll need to see those," Oskar said.

"Help yourself. I have no idea what's there, but himself keeps it in an awful guddle and won't even let me in to dust and polish. Keeps saying he'll do it himself. That's a laugh, and I don't think. I'd be glad to see the back of it all. Nothing but trouble, Arjun is."

"Do you know what was in the safe under the dining room floor, Mrs Morrison?"

"Some of my precious jewellery but one of your lot said there was liquid that had leaked out of something. God alone knows what that was. Gold don't leak."

. . .

Colin and Nadia sat with Mrs Mansoor in the living room while the uniforms implemented the warrant and searched the flat.

Colin looked around at the plush décor and Indian carpets. This home had not been furnished on the cheap. The little woman in the chair opposite him was sitting calmly. She held her hands together and had closed her eyes and was beathing deeply as if to keep out the stress.

"Mrs Mansoor, is there anything that you think we should know about? Anything we might find that you could explain in advance?" Nadia asked.

The woman didn't move.

"I hope she's not dead," Nadia whispered to Colin.

"No, she is not dead, but neither does she want to answer any questions. She does not have to."

"No, you don't Mrs Mansoor. But you might be able to help us," Colin said.

"And why would she want to do that? Her husband is in jail for many years and will be for many more."

"DS Reid, could you come here?"

Colin rose and followed the PC while Nadia sat and watched the other woman close her eyes again and breathe deeply.

"We've found this black box. It was hidden at the bottom of the child's toy box along with these envelopes. The envelopes are full of money and each one has initials and a total written on it. We're getting those counted and bagged now but we can't get this black metal box open."

Colin took the box. "Yuck, it's all wet. It must have leaked from that top, because it's metal, the sides couldn't leak."

"That's what I thought. My guess is something inside has broken, but we can't find a key to get into that."

"I'll ask Mrs Mansoor."

It wasn't long before Colin was back. "She wants to see the box. I'll take it." He carried the black, metal box into the living room. "This is it Mrs Mansoor. Do you know where the key is?"

"Arjun will be most displeased if things are broken. He is a most particular man."

"What's in the box Mrs Mansoor?"

"That I do not know. Indeed, I do not."

"How do we open the box?"

"Carefully," she said. She closed her eyes, joined her hands, and breathed deeply again.

"We found envelopes full of money, too. Why were they in your son's toy box?"

"I know nothing of this."

"It's no use. Just label it all and we'll get the box open at the station," Nadia said.

"I do not think Mr Mansoor will want you to remove his money or that box from his home."

"That's too bad about the money. But about the box, how can you be so sure, if you don't know what's in it?" Nadia asked.

"I know Arjun."

Rachael was beginning to enjoy her role as victim support officer, especially today when she was back at the hospital with Eileen.

"I only met Rory yesterday," Eileen said. "Already I know just where to tickle him behind his ears to please him. Look."

"My goodness, yes, he's certainly enjoying that. What a lovely coat he has. May I pat him?"

"Best not," said Noah. "I'm trying to get him used to Eileen just now, before they start training together."

"No problem. How are you feeling today, Eileen?"

"A little more confident than yesterday. I washed and dressed myself today and brushed my own hair. I had to do it all by feel. What do you think?"

"I think you did well. You look great and you seem to me to be more confident."

"When you are Rory are finished your time together, shall we go downstairs to the canteen for lunch?"

"I'm not sure I'm ready for that."

"I'll tell you what," said Noah. "How about you put on some dark glasses. That's for other people rather than for you. Then we'll all go to the canteen together. You ladies have your lunch, Rory and I will sit with you, and you'll find that everybody will come up and pay attention to Rory. They won't worry about you, Eileen. Trust me. I've seen it hundreds of times."

"Yes, let's try that." Eileen agreed. "I'll hold your arm, Rachael and take my stick. Oh God my heart is pounding, but I must start somewhere.

CHAPTER THIRTY-SEVEN

"You'll be glad to see the back of us, cuz," Jamie said to Frankie.

"Don't think I'm going to say no to that. Cos I won't."

"I don't suppose I could get my bed and a couple of comfy chairs out the house?"

"You're right, you couldn't. That's mine and I'll need it as the girls get bigger and when Harry comes home and the like. There might even be a little Donna sometime. God, I hope it looks like her and not like me."

"Amen to that."

"Fuck off. But I'll give you a hand moving your stuff out of here if you like."

"Good neither of us has a mortgage, eh?"

"Aye well, me pop had to die and yours had to go into the clink to make it happen, but always look on the bright side, Jamie."

"Isn't there a song about that?"

"Fucksake don't sing."

"What the hell's that? Oh. Look. The Morrisons are moving out. Maybe you'll get your keys sooner. That'd be good."

"Here's your hat, what's your hurry. I'm beginning to feel unwanted."

"You don't have a hat, just a balaclava and it never bodes well when you wear that."

"Piss off. Let's get over to the showroom. Is Donna taking the girls to nursery?"

"Aye she'll see us there. Gosh, that removal man's got awfy fancy hair for the job."

"Must be moonlighting," Jamie said. "Look there's the estate agent. Wonder what he wants?"

"Mrs Morrison said he's their nephew so maybe he's brought them the keys to their new house rather than them having to go to the shop."

"How do you know all that?"

"She's a neighbour, we pass the time of day. I'm polite."

"She doesn't pass anything to me, the old battle axe."

"And you're not polite. So there." Frankie shoved his cousin out of the porch and locked the door behind them.

Jamie watched the removers for a moment and noticed that the one with the fancy hair carried lighter unbreakable things like dining chairs and bedside tables.

"That one's definitely moonlighting. I wonder what he really does."

"None of our business, Jamie. Just drive."

Jamie would have been particularly pleased with himself if he had known just how correct his guess was. Paulo McDonald was a waiter at the Pompadour restaurant most days, but since the breakup of his marriage to Lucinda he had to support two homes. That wasn't easy on a waiter's pay. That's why, whenever Burghmuir Removals needed him, he took a shift. It wasn't the best pay in the world, but it was cash in hand, so the Child Support Agency didn't know about it. Usually, the grateful homeowners also provided food and drinks and a cash tip to each of the lads. All good, Paulo jumped down off the van to get another load from the house.

He passed Mr Morrison on the stairs. "Sorry, boss," he said. He stood to the side to let the man pass. Paulo frowned. He'd seen that bloke somewhere before. Where was it?

"Paulo, get a bloody move on," the gaffer shouted.

"Aye, will do." He ran up the stairs two at a time. Where had he seen the owner before? Then he remembered, he worked in his local chemist. No, the new chemist was younger. He'd keep thinking. He picked up a small bookcase and carried it down the stairs.

"It was right nice of you to come all this way to bring us our keys, Hector," Mrs Morrison said. She stood in the living room with her nephew and watched the house empty around her. "It'll be good to be back in Tranent nearer to your mother. Of course, himself'll have further to drive to work, but them's the breaks."

"No problem at all. And you know Mum's expecting you for your tea tonight, don't you? You'll no' feel like cooking after a heavy day lifting and carrying."

"She'll no' be doing any lifting or carrying lad, she'll be supervising and making tea," his uncle complained.

Paulo went into the living room to speak to the woman. "You've forgotten to clear out the fitted wardrobe in the smallest bedroom. It's all full o' papers."

"Bugger, that's Arjun's rubbish. Do we have to take that?" she asked looking at her husband.

"Not if you don't mind telling him why we didn't."

"Look, the gaffer usually charges twenty pounds extra to clear stuff, but how's about you give me a tenner and I'll find a box to put it in and you can decide what to do with it later."

"That's right good of you, son. Give him a tenner." She commanded her husband.

"I ain't got no cash. We paid in advance."

Hector took a tenner out of his wallet and gave it to Paulo. "Thanks mate," he said. Then he took another fifty pounds in ten pound notes out of his wallet. "Give each of the guys a tip when they're done."

"Will do, Hector. He's an old skinflint your uncle is."

Paulo pocketed the money and frowned. He knew the younger one too. Where had he come across him? Of course, if he sold houses, it could be at another removal.

"Paulo, get a fucking shift on." The gaffer shouted.

Paulo picked up a box and raced back up the stairs to empty the forgotten cupboard.

CHAPTER THIRTY-EIGHT

Nadia looked at Colin. "Bloody hell, sarge, does it have to be you and I that are on mugshot duty again?"

"No, Nadia, it's you and me. Aren't we the lucky ones?"

"How come we have to do it?"

"The boss wants someone to go back with the mugshots of those that are still in the frame."

"Who's that then?"

"Felix, Hector and that Morrison fellow who lives next door to Jamie."

"Since when did he come into the mix?"

"Since his house was burgled and..."

"Well, if you ask me, it would make things a whole lot easier if the boss had kept his own rule and never been off duty, rather than mooning over Meera and her engagement ring."

"I didn't ask you, Nadia. Shall we sit and grumble or do our job?"

. . .

Colin and Nadia started in the bar. One member of staff recognised Felix but then disappointed the detectives by saying that he had been in last night. The girl remembered this because he and his friend had gone over to another table where they knew the people, but there had been a bit of a disagreement. His company was not wanted. She did know he had been in before but when he was booking a table he used different names, arrived with a different woman each time and she remembered that he paid cash. That was unusual for their guests. Usually, the meals were paid by card or put on the guests' room. She couldn't help Colin with who had paid for the meal yesterday. She had been in the bar and only looked in briefly during the disagreement. It was loud.

Colin thanked her for her help and he and Nadia walked towards the restaurant.

"He pays in cash. Didn't that waiter tell us Eileen's date had done that?" Nadia asked.

"And he uses different names, Felix, Frederick," Colin said.

The first two members of staff they spoke to hadn't been on duty either last night or the night of Eileen's assault. The maitre d' wasn't in yet because he normally worked the dinner service and the restaurant manager who was on duty earlier hadn't been in at the times in question either.

"Colin, I am rapidly losing the will to live," Nadia said.

Then the manager turned back to them and said, "I see Paulo was working last night. Do you want me to ask him to come through and speak to you?"

"Yes please, that would be most helpful." Colin replied. "Gosh, look at that head of hair, I'm getting hair envy."

"Hmm, it is receding a bit, isn't it?"

"Shut up, Nadia."

"You coppers? Why you looking for me?" Paulo asked.

"We're hoping you might be able to help us," Colin said. "Your manager said you were working here last night."

"She talks too much."

"Do you recognise this man?" Nadia showed him the photo of Mr Morrison. She was surprised when he nodded. "Do you, really?"

"Yes. I said so." Then Paulo lowered his voice. "Don't tell them here, but I've got another job."

"What do you do in this other job?" Colin asked.

"I work with Burghmuir Removals. I was working for this man all day yesterday. I was knackered by the time I did that then I worked here last night"

"What is the man's name?"

"Mr Morrison, that's all I know. But his hair's darker than that. Grecian 2000, I think." Paulo laughed. "And he's let his beard grow a bit. I think he's trying to be trendy, but those days are long behind him."

"Has he ever eaten here?"

"Possibly. I certainly know him from somewhere else apart from yesterday, but I just can't place him. It's been irritating me. I think he's a professional and there's a new pharmacist at my local chemist. At first, I thought it might be him, but it's not. It might be here, I suppose. No, I do know him. I have a new flat since I left my wife." Nadia made a note of his reply. She handed him a card. "Phone me if you remember. Now, what about this man?" She showed him a photo of Hector.

"He's sound, I like him. He made sure Morrison had enough cash to pay us all a good tip. He knows what makes the world go round."

"Has he ever been into the restaurant?" Colin asked.

"Yes, but it was a while ago that I served him. I remember he dined with two women and a man who looked like a fat version of himself. It was funny. The men were clearly trying to impress the women and going on about *darling this and love that*. I remember he paid cash and left a big tip. Just the kind of guest I like."

"What's his name?"

"I'm sorry, I don't remember. Someone who served him more recently would probably recall, but I don't. I do remember he liked guest menus for the other people at his table. He was most particular about that."

"Has he ever been in for dinner alone with a young lady?"

"I'm sure he has, but that's the only time I served at his table. They keep us busy, so I don't have time to clock all the guests."

"What about this man?" Nadia showed Paulo the picture of Felix."

"Is that Sir Felix Buchanan? I hadn't seen him for a while, but he's a pain. He books his tables in different names, but we must remember them and make out like we know him. He comes in with all different women, but we must pretend this is the only one. It's *darling this and that*. I'm amazed they don't see through him and run away."

"When did you see him last?"

"Yesterday, he was a guest at Lord Buchanan's table. Haven't seen either of them for a while before that. Rumour has it Lord Buchanan's been in rehab, but we're not meant to know. They went over to talk to the folk at Dr Myerscough's table, but it was clear they're company wasn't wanted. The maitre d' had to intervene and show the Buchanans to their table. That's how I ended up serving him. I wasn't meant to, but we put them as far away from Dr Myerscough as we could. I thought the big blond man with her was going to land one on Sir Felix and I, for one, didn't fancy his chances of getting back up again."

"Sir Felix likes to wine and dine the ladies here, does he?" Colin asked.

"I doubt many of them are ladies, but he tries to impress by bringing them here."

"Who paid last night?"

"Lord Buchanan. Paid by card but left a decent enough cash tip. He's alright, Lord Buchanan, but Sir Felix is an arse."

Nadia felt like chancing her luck. "Does this man ever eat here?" She showed him a photo of Mansoor.

"Not recently love, he's in the big house, has been for years. Not sure he's the kind of clientele they're looking for as patrons here." Paulo laughed. "Is that all? I better get back to work."

Colin and Nadia thanked him for his help and reminded him to phone Nadia if he remembered anything that might be useful to them.

"Shall we go and take another look at the hotel's CCTV the evening of Eileen's attack?" Nadia asked.

"I was thinking the same thing, but I thought you'd bite my head off."

It took them a while to find the part of the tape they wanted to look at. There was just a glimpse of part of the man's face. But it was around the time that Eileen and Frederick were dining. He was helping a woman to the lifts.

"That could be Frederick and Eileen. It's the right time. It's a pity it's black and white. Look, that's the bit." Nadia paused the film. "Blast, it's gone just too far."

"Run it backwards, frame by frame. I saw it too. There. Stop. Bugger. Forward, one more. Yes."

It was only for a moment, it was only a partial face, but the man did look at the camera.

CHAPTER THIRTY-NINE

Hunter looked around the room. Rachael was missing. She would be with Eileen. She would be a big loss to the team, but he couldn't in all conscience hold her back.

Where was Oskar? Just at that moment the DI entered the room. He explained there had been bad traffic on the Forth Road Bridge across from Fife. Now that he had as full a complement as he was going to get, Hunter called the room to order. Nothing happened. He banged his folder on the desk and shouted at the team to be quiet.

Bear, Mel, and Tim continued munching on bacon rolls in silence while Colin peeled a mandarin. Its scent competed with Hunter's coffee and Bear's bacon to become the dominant smell.

"Please tell me we have made progress," Hunter said.

"I don't know if it's progress, but we have news," Colin said. "Sir Felix Buchanan has admitted to taking cocaine and falling into debt to Mansoor's crowd. When he couldn't pay them back, he was made to take drugs into his gigs for

Mansoor's suppliers and take the money they made to the Morrisons' house in West Mains Road."

"Why not just take it straight to Mrs Mansoor at Mansoor's flat?" Tim asked.

"Firstly, does Mansoor ever do anything the easy way? Secondly, he probably didn't want his wife knowing exactly how much money was involved or Morrison was due a cut of some kind," Colin said.

Tim agreed. "At least we'll get Felix for that."

"He'll probably get a slap on the wrists and a spell in rehab. But that's not our problem. Finding Eileen's attacker is. Who's next?" Hunter asked.

"Mansoor's flat was interesting," Bear said. We found several envelopes of cash with initials on them at the bottom of his child's toy box, along with a black metal box that we couldn't get open."

"The boffins have got it open now. You won't believe what was in it," Hunter said. He looked around the room and said, bottles of fluid for the preservation of bodies and three bottles containing very well-preserved pairs of eyes."

Mel grabbed Colin's bin and vomited her bacon roll into it. "Sorry boss, I've got to..."

"Yes, go and clean yourself up, Mel."

"Yes, we've found the eyes that have been removed from our three victims, one pair of bright blue eyes, one light green and the other Eileen's violet eyes."

"Where did the box come from?" Tim asked.

"Jamie Thomson saw boxes and bottles being moved from the Morrisons' home and followed the van to Mansoor's flat. But we'll need to check for fingerprints and DNA. We can't be sure this is one of the same boxes," Hunter said.

Mel came back into the room.

"You okay now?" Bear asked.

"Good as I'm going to be with that vision in my head."

"Some good news on the horizon is that the charity, Guide Dogs for the Blind has received an anonymous donation of one million pounds." Hunter waited while a gasp went round the room. "The only condition was that Eileen be given the next guide dog to become available, even if she wasn't top of the list. Does anybody here know anything about the donation?" He stared straight at Tim.

"How can we, boss? It was anonymous," Bear said.

"Yes, anonymous." Commented Mel.

"Tim?" Hunter asked.

"Anonymous, boss."

"Aye right, so it was. And we all know better than to tamper with things that are none of our business, don't we?"

"No tampering, boss." Tim smiled. "While we're chatting, could I get a few hours off to take Gillian to the airport? She leaves for Moscow, soon."

"That should be fine, as long as I don't get any information that would lead me to believe you had been tampering, young Myerscough."

"I certainly will not give any such information, boss."

"How did you and Nadia get on at the Waldorf Astoria, Colin?"

"Better than we expected. Felix was identified as having been at the Pompadour yesterday evening. We were told he made a bit of a pest at a table hosted by your sister, Tim and a big blond man looked like he was going to sock it to Felix."

"But not tamper," Tim said.

"No, that's right the word tamper was never used. Felix

was there with Lucky, but Lucky paid on a credit card. The waiter we spoke to recognised Felix as someone who came into the restaurant under a variety of aliases and usually paid cash."

"The interesting thing was that the waiter recognised Mr Morrison and Hector too. Said Hector had been to the pompadour with a fellow who looked like a fat version of himself," Nadia said.

"John." The team chorused.

"Where did he know Mr. Morrison from?" Hunter asked.

"He was moonlighting yesterday with the firm that did his house removal. But he said he knew him from somewhere else and just couldn't place him."

"Well tell him to try a bit harder. I need to know."

"He eventually recalled that Morrison works in the optician's shop near his new flat."

"That holds together. He is an optician," Hunter said.

"Yes boss. We also went back to the night of Eileen's attack and looked again at the CCTV. We found this that we missed before." Nadia handed the picture from the CCTV footage to Hunter.

"Well, I'll be damned."

CHAPTER FORTY

HUNTER ASKED TIM AND BEAR TO COME THROUGH TO HIS ROOM. HE knew they had both known Lucky and Felix since their high school days and hoped they could help him with some background information.

"Take a seat. I've been thinking about the drugs charge we've got on Sir Felix Buchanan, and I want to know why the warrant for his arrest wasn't put out by the Spanish police. Do either of you know?"

"I don't know, boss," Tim said. "But Felix said that if he hadn't left the island double quick the Spaniards would have pursued him. He told me there was a misunderstanding with a Spanish girl and some coke was found at his gig and the Spanish police believed he was responsible."

"But it was all a misunderstanding. He just didn't take any chances, in case he couldn't make himself understood," Bear said. "Although my guess is that someone in the Spanish police force on Ibiza speaks English."

"I agree Bear. Could Lucky have bribed someone to drop this?"

"Unlikely, boss. Lucky is a tight wad at the best of times, and he has a lot of land and a big house, but not too much ready cash."

"I agree with Bear, boss."

"Does Felix have money?"

"I don't know, he was a year or so younger than Bear and I and of course they went to Fettes."

"Yes, but for God's sake, the Ambassador's son and the Chief Constable's boy who's a wealthy heir, you all mixed in the same circles."

"I know Felix's family have money. They run art galleries in London and all the world cities, so if someone was paid to ignore Felix's indiscretions, the family could have arranged that."

"Let me phone the Spaniards while you're here. I want to find out if Felix displayed violence towards that woman while he was in Ibiza and whether he was known to have been under the influence of cocaine, or any other substance, at the time."

CHAPTER FORTY-ONE

"You would think that when someone moves house they would take all their stuff with them, wouldn't you Frankie?"

"Why should I think that? You didn't. You tried to nick me dining room chairs, me comfy recliners and me kettle but left all your crappy DVDs and your toaster that doesn't work. If you've got to hire a skip to get rid of the Morrisons' rubbish, that's karma, cuz. Pure karma. Oh, and I've put your toaster in there just in case you were wondering."

"Are you going to stop moaning long enough to give me a hand?"

"Aye, all right. Where do you want me to start?"

"You start in the garage, and I'll start in the kitchen."

Frankie wandered over to the garage and opened the door. "Fucksake, Jamie. It's rammed. What do you want me to throw?"

"All of it, every last bit."

Frankie rolled up his sleeves and began the long process of clearing the space. There were half used tins of paint, bits of wood, rusted tools and a bicycle with one wheel and no handlebars. He just kept going, moving a little further into the space every time he got rid of something.

After a couple of hours, he went into the house for a pee and a drink and found Jamie tearing the old-fashion kitchen units off the walls.

"I'm stopping for a drink and a bag of crisps. Want anything?"

"Aye, a beer and any flavour but salt and vinegar."

"We don't have any salt and vinegar."

"Good. I don't like them. How you getting on?"

"Can't believe they thought the place was empty with all that stuff in there."

"Wait till you see the attic."

"At least they took their bits and pieces out of the kitchen, and you can get to clearing it. Who you getting to put the new one in?"

"Perfectly Good Kitchens and Bathrooms."

"I hope they're right or we'll get them under the trades descriptions. We'll not get all this done today, Jamie. I hope you know that."

"Luckily there are two days in the weekend, and I've closed the showroom on Monday."

"I hope your pop doesn't hear about that."

"Are you going to tell him?"

"Not a fucking chance, but it wouldn't surprise me if he finds out anyway. I've got another couple of hours in the garage, then I'm stopping for lunch."

"Lunch?"

"Donna's made some sandwiches. Looks like she did enough for both of us."

"Good woman. Let's meet back here in two hours."

"You make it sound like we're James Bond or something, no' just two cousins sitting on your living room carpet. See you then."

Frankie went back to the garage, there were bottles of turpentine, that he emptied onto the ground before throwing the bottles onto the skip, Hard, old paint brushes matted with different colours and gardening tools, all of which had seen better days.

Then he finally made it to the shelf at the back of the garage. There was a large box of books that was bloody heavy. He decided to take the books out and throw them into the skip in small bundles. There was no point in asking Jamie if he wanted any of them, he'd never read a book in his life and was unlikely to start now.

First there were bundles of Mills and Boon romances. Maybe Linda might like them. No, she had enough to worry about with Eileen. He'd just toss them. Then there were a set of westerns, they looked quite exciting, but went the way of the romances anyway.

The next pile were classics reprinted with modern covers. Frankie noticed none of them looked like they had ever been opened, he couldn't blame the Morrisons for that. They looked right boring: Bleak House, Barnaby Rudge and Hard Times. Ye gods.

Right at the bottom of the box were heavier books. Frankie took them out one at a time. They looked like textbooks: The Physiology of the Eye, The Anatomy of the Head, The Eye Surgeon's Hand Book. Oh Fuck. Throw them out like he hadn't seen them or show Jamie?

The decision was taken out of his hands when Jamie

walked into the garage. "Where are these sandwiches, then, Frankie Boy? What's that? What the fuck?"

Jamie stared at the books with his mouth wide open. He flicked through one of them and put it back on the shelf.

"We can't unsee it, can we?" Frankie asked.

"No, we bloody can't. But I want to have lunch while we work out what to do next."

"You don't want me to throw these out, then?"

"No, keep the eye books, but don't leave them where Linda'll see them."

"I'll leave them in the box in the garage. They might just be old Morrison's books from when he was studying to become an optician, you know."

"They might. You going up into the attic after lunch?"

"Aye. You done in the kitchen?"

"Yep. I'm going to rip up the carpets next. That should be fun."

"You need to get out more."

"Not much chance of that. Linda wants this place sorted jig time. Any more to eat? I'm ravenous."

"A couple of apples and a packet of jaffa cakes. You can have the apples."

"That'll happen."

After lunch Jamie set to work on the carpets and floor coverings. He wondered how many valuables the Morrisons had. He found a safe under the floor in the kitchen and another under the dining room. He was pondering this when the door-bell rang.

"Imran, Perfectly Good Kitchens and Bathrooms," the man said.

"I thought you weren't starting till tomorrow."

"We have it down for installation starting tomorrow. I'm here to take everything out today."

"Great, but I've already got all the cupboards out of the kitchen."

"Good, then this should be quick. You're not living here, are you?" Imran asked.

Jamie laughed. "You're joking, right?"

"You'd be surprised. I have to ask before I turn off the water and disconnect the loo."

"I'd offer you a cuppa, but I've got no electricity on right now."

"No worries, I'll finish off the kitchen then strip out the bathroom suite. It won't take me long because you've done so much."

"Jamie, look what I've found."

Jamie saw a mummified mouse whirl to the ground. "What the fuck, Frankie?"

"What's that?" Imran asked.

"I've found a whole load of stuffed dead animals up here. They're gross. But some of them are huge. There's a fox as well as a badger. I can't carry them down the ladder. I'll need to throw them down." Frankie called out.

"No, you bloody won't. I don't want them splitting and the stuffing going all over the floor. I'll come up. You can hand them to me one by one." Jamie shouted back.

"I'll leave you to it. I'll be in the kitchen if you need me," Imran said.

Jamie helped Frankie with all the stuffed animals. Each one

appeared to be more grotesque than the last. There was a ginger cat, a magpie, a fish that hadn't taken properly and was manky as well as the animals Frankie had identified earlier. There was also another box of books, mainly about taxidermy and preservation of dead bodies, a chest of old clothes, an old bedframe that the woodworms had enjoyed and two suitcases that were so old, they didn't have wheels.

The two men threw everything into the skip and came back in to finish pulling up the flooring.

"Is it safe for me to start on the bathroom? You're not going to throw any more dead animals about, are you?" Imran asked Frankie.

"No. Sorry mate, I didn't know you were here. Just thought I'd shake Jamie up a bit."

"I think you managed that for both of us," Imran said. He bounded up the stairs and soon started work on removing the sink.

"There's a whole lot of bottles of solution in the cupboard under the sink. It says it's embalming fluid," Imran said. "Do you need that, Jamie?"

"Yuck no."

"Or maybe yes," Frankie said.

"I'm phoning Tim. This is getting creepy."

CHAPTER
FORTY-TWO

"DC Grant as I live and breathe. You just won't give up, will you Mel? Me and Linda are tight, and you're just going to have to get used to that."

"You're a funny man, Jamie. But perhaps you've found something left in your new house by the previous owners that is not so humorous."

"He found nothing. He had me clearing out the garage and then had me up in the loft amongst the spiders and the creepy dead animals, but he wants all the glory," Frankie said.

"Shut it Frankie, we've both been hard at it."

"Aye, true enough."

"What did you find?" Tim asked.

"Well, it may be something and nothing, but thinking about what happened to Eileen, Jamie and I thought we should tell you."

"See these books, here?" Jamie asked. "Frankie came across them in the garage. They're all about eyes and operating on eyes and the like."

"That's not too surprising, Jamie, Mr Morrison is a qualified optician. He's bound to have studied the eyes and everything to do with them. Let me take a look," Mel said. She flicked through each book in turn and then handed them on to Tim.

"I can see why you would be concerned," Tim said, "But these are all textbooks."

"But why would he need to know about surgery to the eyes. Opticians just look, don't they?" Jamie asked.

"Yes, but although they don't carry out surgery, they are highly qualified and often spot diseases not even associated with the eye. That's why they carry out so many tests before you're prescribed a pair of specs."

"Well put that together with the taxidermy animals Frankie found in the attic," Jamie said.

"Aye they're really creepy. I didn't half make Jamie jump when I threw down a deed mouse."

"I did not jump. I was just playing along."

"Where abouts were they in the attic, Frankie?" Mel asked.

"Right at the back. All shadowy and stinky. It's pure gross."

"It's not my kind of thing either," Tim said. "But there's nothing illegal about enjoying the art of taxidermy. Again, it's a skilful pursuit."

"Your no' much for going after Morrison, are you Blondie?"

"You've given me nothing to go after him with, Jamie."

"Well, what about this embalming fluid, suitable for human and animal body parts."

"Good Lord, man. If his hobby was taxidermy, of course he would need that for the animals he was working on." Tim looked at Jamie and Frankie. He could see the frustration on their faces. "Look, guys, I'm sorry. I just don't think there's anything here. It's not enough."

"We are doing our level best to find out who assaulted Eileen, and I promise that won't stop," Mel said. "But none of this helps."

"Hey Jamie, your old lady make fancy cake decorations, does she?" Imran came down the stairs from the bathroom. "I found this old bottle under the bath. These must have been for Halloween, I'd guess." In his hand he carried a dusty jar.

"Linda couldn't make a fancy cake if her life depended on it, mate," Jamie said.

He took the jar from Imran and almost dropped it. Tim caught it before it crashed onto the floor.

"Now you have enough."

CHAPTER
FORTY-THREE

Mel had never seen Jamie move so fast as when Tim asked him if he had a forwarding address for Mr and Mrs Morrison. He ran out of his new house into the front garden and vaulted the fence onto Frankie's ground. In moments he was back in front of the detectives with a scrap of paper in his hand. He handed it to Mel.

"They've moved to Tranent. Isn't that where John used to live, Tim?"

"Yes, I believe most of his family still do."

"I'll phone the station and get someone out to pick him up," Mel said.

Mel was glad to hear Bear's voice answer the phone in the incident room. She told him what Imran had found, but he was not surprised.

"The fingerprint analysis came back from that black box," he said. "The boffins found traces of prints from Mr Morrison. Luckily, you and Oskar insisted on getting those for comparison during the burglary."

"It's all that made sense. So, we've got a slam dunk if his prints have been identified."

"Not really, fingerprints belonging to Hector, Felix and Mrs Mansoor have also been found."

"Bloody hell. But a wee woman like Mrs Mansoor never could have carried out the murders or the attack on Eileen, surely?" Mel asked.

"Probably not, but it still leaves Arjun Mansoor with a possible part in the crimes. You know how manipulative he is."

"Yep. Anyway, will you get your booty over to Tranent and pick up Morrison? He has some questions to answer."

"I'll check with the boss. He may want someone more senior to go, but I'll sort it, pet."

"Thanks. And it's left-over lasagne and salad for tea," she said.

"And chips?"

"With pasta? I don't think so, big man."

Bear went through to Hunter's office to tell him of the finds. Hunter sat and listened to the DC as the finds in Jamie's new house were revealed. He heard about the books and took a sharp intake of breath.

"Yes, but Mr Morrison is an optician, boss," Bear said.

"Did nobody think to impart this gem of knowledge to me? This makes his position worse, not better. He understands the structure of the eyes and has books on the subject."

"Surely, he would have had books to allow him to study his profession, boss. The same with the embalming fluid for preservation of human and animal body parts."

"You what?" Hunter roared.

"It seems his hobby was taxidermy. So, he would need that."

"I suppose."

"But now the plumber has found a dusty jar hidden under the bath with a pair of eyes floating in it..."

"You find Oskar and bring bloody Morrison to me. I'll give him eyes in a dusty jar. Go Bear. Now."

Oskar and Bear took one of the pool cars to drive out to East Lothian. Bear drove to give Oskar the chance to look at the view and think. Bear took the A1 because, although it was not the prettiest route, it was the fastest way to get from Edinburgh to Tranent.

"What do we know about our four owners of the sets of fingerprints?" Oskar asked Bear.

"You tell me. I'm driving."

"We know that Morrison knows Arjun Mansoor and rates him and his interest in and knowledge of eyes. That is important to Morrison because that's his professional interest."

"Yep. And Felix knows Mansoor, because he was his drug dealer and Felix was indebted to him and did work for him."

"Do we know if Hector knows Mansoor?"

"I'm guessing he at least knows of him. Mansoor is John's drug dealer, remember."

"Of course. Mrs Mansoor knows Arjun because she's married to him." Oskar smiled.

"Lucky lady, isn't she?"

"Right, let's turn our attention to Felix. He knows Mr Morrison and Arjun Mansoor because he has to deliver envelopes of drug money to Morrison for Mansoor. But does he know Hector?"

"No reason why he should. I mean, Hector will probably know of the Buchanan family because Lucky's estate crosses into East Lothian where Hector lives and works. He may even know of Felix's branch of the family because they are wealthy."

"But Felix is not."

"No. Any money he gets, he shoves up his nose."

"Still, we do not know that Felix knows Hector and we do not think he does."

"Correct. But Hector knows Morrison and probably knows of Mansoor through his brother."

"And Mrs Mansoor, who does she know?"

"Apart from her husband, she'll know Morrison, because he was the delivery man for the money. No reason why she would know either Felix or Hector," Bear said. "Here we are in Tranent, keep your eyes open for the turn."

Bear didn't think Mr Morrison looked surprised to see them. The man got into the car without a fuss and sat silently in the back, beside Oskar all the way as Bear drove back to Fettes Station.

"Interview room one is free," Charlie said.

"Thanks, Sarge," Bear led Mr Morrison into the interview room.

Charlie sent through a PC to stand inside the room at the door until the interview began. Bear looked at him. He seemed to Bear to be about twelve years old.

Charlie noticed Bear looking. "Yes, they are getting younger. And I retire in eighteen pay checks."

"Something for us all to look forward to."

"Don't you start. I get enough of that off bloody Hunter."

"Enough of what?" Hunter asked. He had come downstairs into reception and overheard the end of the conversation.

"Cheek," Charlie said.

"Bear, Oskar is going to interview Morrison with me. Could you bring us three coffees out of the machine?"

"Are you sure, boss? It tastes of dust."

"I know, but I'm not giving my good stuff to that man."

"We don't know he's done anything yet."

"Just bring it through."

"Yes boss."

"I prefer tea," Morrison said.

"Tell someone who cares," Hunter said.

He ran through the taping of the interview and advised Morrison that he was being interview under caution with regard to two murders and an attempted murder, all of which involved the removal of the victim's eyeballs.

Morrison sat and looked at the table. "Can I get a lawyer?"

"If you think you need one."

"Oh God, I don't know."

"Well, while you think about it, can you tell me if that is you in this photograph."

Morrison frowned at the photo. "I don't have my specs with me. I can't see properly. Where was it taken? I don't recognise the place."

"It was taken in the Waldorf Astoria Hotel just after that man and the woman he's supporting had eaten in the Pompadour Restaurant there," Hunter said.

"No that can't be me then. I've never been in that hotel and I certainly can't afford to eat there."

"So, you can see the surroundings clearly enough that you know you don't recognise them, but you don't recognise yourself," Oskar said.

"Because that's not me."

Hunter read out the dates of the two murders, as far as Meera had been able to deduce them, and the date of the attack on Eileen. Then asked Mr. Morrison where he had been on those occasions.

"I don't know. I don't have my diary with me, and they took my phone at the desk. But I don't go out much. I was probably at home with my wife."

"Do you know the woman called Eileen Maguire?"

"No."

"Have you ever used a dating website?"

"Have you met my missus? It'd be more than my life's worth."

"Do you have an interest in taxidermy?"

"What?"

"Taxidermy." Hunter repeated. "The preserving and stuffing of dead animals and birds."

"I know what it is. It's revolting. The wife's father was into it. We've got a whole lot of his spooky old treasures in the loft at West Mains Road." The man laughed. "I left them there for Jamie Thomson. I hope they scare the bejesus out of him when he finds them."

"It did." Hunter smiled. "Have you ever been involved in any assaults that resulted in the removal of another person's eyes?"

"God no! I've never hurt anybody in my life. Especially not eyes. I like eyes. I help to save them, not harm them."

"Do you know of anybody who has shown a greater than normal interest in eyes, your work or the preservation of body parts?" Oskar asked.

The man took a drink of his coffee, then stared again at the table. When he looked up again, he had tears in his eyes. "I think I should call that lawyer now."

"He didn't have his own lawyer, Andrew, that's why we called you," Hunter said.

"Okay. Let me have a few minutes with him. Then I'll give you a shout."

Hunter nodded and opened the door for Andrew Barley before introducing him to his new client.

"Oskar and I will be upstairs. Shall we come back in fifteen minutes?"

"That should do us. And two teas, if you can. They're not quite as revolting as the coffee in your machines."

Hunter smiled, asked the PC to get the teas and then he followed Oskar upstairs to the incident room. Rachael was sitting on Nadia's desk while Colin sat on the chair next to it.

"I think that's a clever idea. Why don't you put it to the boss, Rache?"

"Rachael, do you have an idea?"

"Yes boss. It's just that I went to see Eileen again today."

"How's she getting on with the guide dog."

"She's still getting used to him and they'll have to do a lot of training together, but at least she likes him now. She trusts him too."

"Good. Did she remember anything else that might help us?" Hunter asked.

"Perhaps. She said that Frederick always called her 'darling' and nobody else had ever called her darling."

"How does that help us?"

"She told me that he used a particular tone and that, with the timbre of his voice sent shivers down her spine and made her feel gooey inside. She's sure she'd recognise his voice if she heard it saying *darling*, or *Eileen darling* or *darling Eileen*. I thought it might be worth a try to record our remaining suspects and see if she can identify Frederick by his voice."

"Rachael don't tell Jane, but I love you. That's a great idea."

"Janey's in no danger, boss."

"Come on, Oskar, we're late for a date with Mr. Morrison."

"Just give me a minute. I need to speak to DC Chan."

Nadia looked up from her computer screen. "Can I help?"

"I'm told that you and Colin are the best paper chasers on the team."

"We do have an eye for detail, if I can use that phrase in this case. What's up?"

"Could you contact The General Optical Council for me and find out when Mr. Morrison qualified as an optician? I'd like to know if he's kept his post-qualification education up to date too."

"Shouldn't take long. I'll get it done." Nadia smiled

Oskar followed Hunter down the stairs and found him at reception asking Charlie to find him a little recording device.

"You know you can record on your phone now, Hunter. These devices are amazing."

"I do know that smart arse, but I want something separate."

He opened the door of interview room one. And saw Andrew Barley nod to him.

"My client is ready to answer more questions."

"The last question I asked that your client has failed to answer was this: Mr Morrison, can you think of anybody who has shown a greater than normal interest in eyes, your work or the preservation of body parts?" Oskar asked.

"Arjun Mansoor was always interested in what I did. I originally met him when he came in as a patient to the optician's shop I work in. He came in for his eye examinations and would talk to me about the structure of the eyeball, how it was situated in the head and the protection it got from the bony socket in the skull."

"Did you find that odd?"

"Not at first. Many people are interested in eyes. They are said to be the window of the soul and all that. But then he began to ask about different colours of eyes. His are dark brown. I told him that brown is the most common colour of eyes. That didn't please him much. He became quite angry."

"Really?"

"Yes, as if I were saying he was common. I had to quickly explain myself and tell him how eye colour was determined by the amount of melanin produced in the body."

"Did that calm him down?" Hunter asked.

"Oh yes. But then he wanted to know which colours of eyes were least common and most distinctive. We had long chats about that. He was fascinated and I enjoyed sharing my knowledge."

"How did that interest develop?" Oskar asked.

"I suppose it was from those discussions that things became uncomfortable. He wanted to know if eyes could be removed from a corpse. I told him they probably could but that there are no reflexes after death, so the pupils don't react to light and the cornea becomes a bit cloudy within two hours of the person dying."

"What did Mansoor say to that?"

"He told me he would like to have an example of each of the rarest colours of eyes and asked if the eyes were removed from a living person, would they keep their colour."

"I said they might if they were correctly treated, but I thought probably not. Then I laughed and said that I could not imagine anybody being willing to supply specimens for such a collection." Morrison looked at Hunter and said, "but he didn't laugh."

"What were the eyes doing hidden under the bath of your old home?" Oskar asked.

"Oh fuck, I forgot about those. I'd hidden them from the wife." Morrison looked at Andrew Barley and asked, "shall I just tell them?"

"You might as well, you've gone this far."

"Mansoor brought me a dead cat."

"But he's in jail," Hunter said.

"This was years ago. He wanted to watch while I removed the eyes and then preserved them. He noted down every detail. He wanted to know if the process would be the same for a human eye and I confirmed that it would be much the same. I hid them because the sight of the eyes would upset my wife. She loves cats."

"But Arjun Mansoor has been in jail for a long time now. He was not involved in the murders earlier in the year, nor was he able to take part in the assault on Eileen Maguire. Did you continue with his work to allow him to expand his collection?"

"God no! On my mother's life I never did."

"My guess is you mother has been dead for an easy ten

years," Oskar said. "So that promise won't count for much.

"What did you do, Mr Morrison?" Hunter asked.

"If a pair of eyes came to me, my job was to preserve them. That is all."

"You didn't think to ask any questions?" Oskar asked.

"Who brought you the eyes, Mr. Morrison?" Hunter asked quietly.

CHAPTER
FORTY-FOUR

Linda was already with Eileen when Rachael arrived at the hospital.

"Where are Noah and Rory this morning?" Rachael asked.

"They'll be here soon. I'm going to move into a rehabilitation centre in a day or two. I'll get used to looking after myself and I have to learn to go out and about with Rory to guide me."

"You're doing really well already, sis. I'm amazed."

"To be honest, I've amazed myself and I'll be quite glad to get out of here. The nurses are lovely, but the food is boring and I'm always too hot."

"I think, if you are complaining about the food, you are ready to leave hospital." Rachael sat down on a chair beside Eileen's bed and took her hand. "There is something I want to ask you."

"Oh dear, is it something bad?"

"No. But it is something you could do for us to help find your attacker, but only if you feel up to it. You must say no if the idea is too upsetting for you."

"What on earth is it, Rachael?"

"If we recorded the men under investigation saying 'darling' and 'Eileen darling' and 'darling Eileen', would you feel able to listen to them all and tell us if you recognised any of the voices as being Frederick's"

"Yes. Yes of course. That's a brilliant idea. I really could help that way."

Linda frowned. "Eileen, this is a fine idea, and I know you want to help, but it could also be immensely stressful and scary to hear that man saying those things again. You must say no if you don't feel up to it."

"I know, Linda. But I do. I know it will be spooky hearing his voice again, but this way I can help and not just sit around like a couch potato, or worse still, a victim. I don't want to be a victim; I want to be me."

"This is such good news. You're the bravest person I know, Eileen," Rachael said.

"So much of the time I just sit about feeling low and wondering why this happened to me. What terrible thing must I have done in a past life to justify losing my eyes. Not just my sight, my eyes. I must look dreadfully ugly now."

"You really don't," Rachael said quickly. "I'll be honest, just after your operation, your eye socket looked red, and you had swelling and bruises too."

"I'm not surprised after all my poor eyes sockets had been through."

"Exactly," Linda said. "It's much better now. Do you think you'll get prosthetic eyes fitted?"

"I'll see what the doctors say, but unless it's to keep the shape of my face, I don't think there's any point. I still won't be able to see. Because of the damage to my face around my eyes, I think I'll get a larger pair of dark glasses. No so much for me, but so that I don't frighten people who have to look at me."

"That's your choice, Eileen, but you must never blame yourself for that man's wickedness," Rachael said.

"These boys aren't frightened of you, lady," Noah walked into the room. He let Rory's leash go and the dog ran to Eileen, wagging his tail. "Don't be fooled, that's not love. I told him you have dog treats."

Eileen reached towards her bedside cabinet, opened the little door at the front and took out two bags. She felt them and put the bag of chocolate eclairs back before taking a couple of treats out of Rory's bag.

"Here you go, boy. Good dog. Another one? Oh, go on then. I'm glad you chose Rory for me. He's lovely."

"Were you talking about dark glasses as I walked in?" Noah asked.

"Yes, I thought I'd get a larger pair to cover up most of the disfigurement around my eye sockets."

"It's a good idea for a couple of other reasons too."

"What are they?" Eileen asked.

"You have to remember that if you go outside without prosthetic eyes, the skin and scars in your eye sockets will be very tender and susceptible to sunlight. The last thing you want is to get that part of your face burned."

"Gosh, I never thought of that," Linda said. "You will have to be careful, sis."

"The other reason is really as a warning to others that you can't see. If you walk around in a supermarket or a shopping mall, people tend to look at eye level. They may not immediately notice Rory, or a white stick if you use one but you can draw attention to your lack of sight by wearing dark glasses. It often helps keep you safe, especially if the place you need to go is crowded and you might bump into other people or things."

"What you say all makes good sense, Noah. I'll do that."

"Now, enough of this gassing. Let's go for a little stroll outside with Rory. You'll learn to use his harness soon enough, but for now, I'll take your arm." Noah touched Eileen lightly on her left arm and she put it through his. "Hold the lead in your right hand and keep Rory on a short leash inside. If Rachael walks ahead of us and Linda a couple of steps behind, you will have your security ring around you."

"Who would have thought a short walk in the hospital grounds could be this exciting?" Eileen giggled. "Did I tell you my work phoned today?"

"No, what did they say?"

"Instead of having incoming calls going to any phone that's free, they're going to streamline things and have a telephone receptionist who can answer minor queries or put the calls to the correct person as appropriate."

"That sounds like a good use of resources," Rachael said.

"And I've been offered the job of telephone receptionist as soon as I'm well enough to go back to work. I even get a pay rise."

"That's excellent," Noah said. He patted her hand that was folded around his arm. "But you do know that it will take some time to adapt to your new life, don't you?"

"Yes. But I'm so pleased to have a new job to look forward to. And I liked my colleagues, or at least I was used to them."

Rachael laughed. "I hear you, Eileen," she said. "Your life going forward will be different to the way you expected it to be, but it will go on, and I have a feeling that you're going to be fine."

CHAPTER FORTY-FIVE

HUNTER BANGED THE DESK WITH HIS FIST. "LET'S GET DOWN TO business. We are so close to nailing this monster that I want it done. Oskar, can you report on our meeting with Mr Morrison yesterday?"

"Yes. I can do that, Hunter. Mr Morrison told us a lot. Not all of it was true, but he said a lot." The Polish DI smiled at his new colleagues before he continued. "Steven Frederick Morrison, born in Glasgow September tenth nineteen hundred and seventy-eight."

"Frederick?" Colin asked.

"He's not as old as he looks," Mel said.

"You'd look older if you lived with Mrs Morrison, believe me." Tim joked.

"Look at Meera. I heard she's only twenty-six, but with all the time she spends with the boss, she could easily pass for ten years older." Bear chuckled.

"Go on, Oskar, ignore them," Hunter said.

"He told the boss and me a long story about Mansoor and how his relationship with him grew and the interest Mansoor took in his work. Now, I haven't met Mansoor, but all I've read about him and heard about him from all of you, Mansoor is interested in two things, money and power. If he appeared interested in Morrison's work, it had to be useful to him for one of those purposes."

"I agree, Oskar, and let's face it, the story we were told was wildly complicated. My thoughts are that no more than half of it is true."

"But which half?"

"I may be able to help with a bit that wasn't true," Nadia said. "You asked me to check the register held by The General Optical Council, Oskar. And surprise, surprise, our friend Steven Frederick Morrison has never been on it."

"What?" Hunter looked at Nadia in surprise. "He works for a most respected optician. The company operates all over the country."

"Yes, he does. But he never qualified."

"And nobody ever checked?"

"Oh, I don't doubt he has some kind of certificate, but he probably forged it."

"Now that would make sense. If Mansoor found out about that, it would give him power over Morrison. Good thinking, Oskar and well done, Nadia."

"There is one more thing, boss," Nadia said. "After that result, I contacted the U.K. Guild of Taxidermists. Mr. Morrison joined two years ago after completing a course in the craft at The British Academy of Taxidermy."

"All that waffle about the interest in taxidermy being his father-in-law's was just hogwash." Hunter growled.

"If that's what he said, it seems to have been untrue," Nadia said.

"Apart from the fact that Morrison is a liar, what else have we learned?" Hunter asked.

"What did he say about Hector helping him to move all that stuff from his old house to Mansoor's flat?" Tim asked.

"Bugger, I forgot about that. We didn't ask." Hunter looked sheepish. "But as we're going to arrest him now, we can ask him then."

"He did admit to preserving eyes that were brought to him, but I doubt now there's much truth in that."

"Who did he claims brought them to him?" Mel asked.

"He coughed up Hector Hamilton's name," Oskar said.

"I wouldn't be surprised. John's a bad lot. And that CCTV photo Nadia and I got at the hotel could very well be Hector, but I can't be sure. I wish it were clearer," Colin said.

"And Morrison is such a nice guy, to drop his own family in it," Oskar said. "But Hector's coming in this morning to answer more questions. It may be just what we need for the family members to turn against each other and get the truth that way."

"I have good news," Rachael said.

"Excellent, that's what we need," Hunter said.

"Eileen has agreed to listen to tapes of the voices of the different men, she is confident she'll be able to recognise Frederick that way."

"Great. I've got the tape of Morrison saying the agreed phrases. Oskar, you and Neil interview Hector when he comes in and get him to repeat them and Tim, will you and Bear go out to speak to Felix and get him to repeat them?"

"No can do, boss. I'm taking Gillian to the airport today for the first leg of her journey to Moscow."

"Sorry, Tim. I forgot. Bear, you and Mel make arrangements to go out to Sir Felix, will you?"

"Yes, boss. No problem. Is there anyone else still in the frame?"

"No, but just for comparison, Colin, you and Nadia go out to Saughton and get Mansoor to say the words. Ask him about his eye-sight too, will you?"

"Yes, boss."

"Rachael, are you going over to spend time with Eileen again today?"

"Yes, boss. She's moving from the hospital to the rehab facility where she'll learn how to live as a blind person. She's excited about it, but nervous too."

"I'm not surprised. Imagine just waking up one morning and such a fundamental sense has been taken from you. I'm delighted she's willing to listen to the voices."

"She's brave and thrilled to think she can truly help. That we're not just making this job up for her. Oh, and her work have told her she has a job with them as soon as she's well enough to go back. That made a real difference to her mood too. She wants to be useful and look forward."

"Don't we all?"

Bear looked into Hunter's office. "Boss, I phoned the Buchanan estate and McKellar answered the phone. But when he went to get Felix, he said I'd just missed him. He'd gone out."

"Did you say why you wanted to see him?"

"Not specifically, just that we needed a few more details from him. It was too complicated to explain why we wanted him to repeat a few phrases."

"Did McKellar say where he'd gone?"

"No boss, just that we'd missed him."

"Okay, Bear, keep trying. Do you have Felix's mobile number?"

"No, but I think Tim has it."

"Terrific. Phone young Myerscough and see what you can do."

More bloody interviews. I have spent enough time being grilled by police officers. I try not to lie, but I can't tell the whole truth. Enough really is enough. What else can they possibly want to ask me?

I needed out, away from here. After all, I've done some bad things, but it wasn't really me. I had no choice. It was never my idea. I was made to do it, and how could I know they would die? Actually, it might be better if they'd all died.

And that stuff in the house. Why oh why was it not moved on to Mansoor's house sooner? Why leave it to the last minute. Why let anybody else know about it? Fucking idiot. I really am a fucking idiot.

I should never have agreed to Mansoor's terms. But I did, and now it feels like there's no way out. I need to get away. East Lothian may not be far enough.

CHAPTER
FORTY-SIX

When Tim arrived back at the house, Gillian's luggage was in the hall. There was so much of it that he immediately knew he would have to take his big BMW. The Mercedes was built for speed, not moving so many of Gillian's belongings.

He found her in the morning room deep in conversation with his father. They had never been particularly close but had clearly found common ground today.

"No, I won't forget you, Sir Peter. Anyway, my contract is only for a year. I'll be back sooner than you know."

"Are you ready to go? You don't want to miss your flight," Tim said.

"Yes, I'm ready, Tim. But this one's only to Heathrow. I have a few hours before my flight from London to Moscow."

"Why leave so early?" Sir Peter asked.

"I have to change terminals, and I don't want to rush when I'm traveling on my own."

"Safe journey, dear," Sir Peter said. He kissed her lightly on the green flash in her hair and smiled.

Tim turned back to the hall. “Is all this your luggage? How much excess do you have?” He laughed.

“None, you bought me a first-class ticket with benefits, remember? And I better give this back to you.” Gillian handed the black, limitless American Express card to Tim.

“No, just keep it in case you need it, pet,” he said.

“I’d feel guilty about taking it with me. What if I lost it, or it got stolen? Please take it back Tim.”

“Then it will be waiting for you when you return. And I can always get a new card issued for you if you do need it. Just let me know.”

“You’re a good man.”

“Enough of all that, let’s get you out of here. Kenneth, could you help me with the luggage.”

Tim smiled as Kenneth appeared as if from nowhere and lifted two of the smaller bags.

“I’m not as young as I used to be,” he said.

Tim’s father dragged a stuffed roller bag onto the drive beside the car, and Tim carried two cases that were deceptively heavy. “What on earth have you got in here? Is Alice in one of these cases?”

“Indeed I am not, Master Timothy. My old bones wouldn’t fold up into that little space anymore.” The cook came out to wave Gillian off. “Stay safe and enjoy your new post, Miss Gillian,” she said.

Goodbyes and good wishes exchanged, Gillian climbed into the car and looked at Tim.

“I didn’t think this would be quite so hard,” she said.

Without saying a word, Tim put the car in gear and began the drive to the airport. He parked in the multi storey carpark and found a trolley to allow him to push the luggage across to the airport terminal.

"If you find you've forgotten anything." He began.

"I'll buy it there." Gillian smiled. "I'm going to Moscow, not Mars, Tim."

"I know, I know."

He stood back and watched her load her luggage onto the conveyor belt. He knew she was already checked in. Heather at the travel agents had seen to all that.

"Checked in all the way to Boryspil International Airport," Gillian said. "That's a relief. Shall we have a coffee before I head for security?"

"I'd like that." He walked beside her to the Café Nero. It was the only coffee shop he could see landside at the airport, although he suspected there must be others. The coffee really didn't matter, time with Gillian before she left did.

There were several tables available. They stopped at one in a secluded corner where they would not be easily seen.

"Bonus. It's been cleaned," Gillian said.

Tim worked out that they were well hidden and could have a quiet chat and a kiss before Gillian left. He was going to miss her.

"What can I get you?"

"Cappuccino for me, Tim, with lots of chocolate."

He smiled. "Old habits die hard."

"It's harder to get a really good coffee over there," she said. "I tend to drink the tea. It's usually better."

Tim went up to the counter. He decided to get two cookies to go with the coffee. Just then he felt a tap on his shoulder.

"Hello, Tim, I thought it was you. I arrived far too early for my flight, so I thought I'd just stop for a coffee before I catch my plane to Dublin. Another gig, you know."

"Hi Felix. Dublin. Great city. It's too long since I've been."

"You should come along to my gig. I could show you around."

"Not this time. I'm only here to see Gillian off on her way to Moscow. She secured a teaching post there for a year. Leaves today."

"I remember she said she was going soon when we met up at the Pompadour. It occurred to me that we might be travelling on the same day. May I join you?"

Tim couldn't think of a polite way to say no. "Sure, we're at that table there." He put their coffees on his tray.

"Good I'll come over," Felix said. "Oh, where are my manners? Let me get these. Leave the tray and I'll put mine on there too. I'll get this."

"There's really no need."

"I insist. My absolute pleasure. Ooh. Cookies. Good idea. I'll follow you over."

Tim walked back to the table. "Felix Buchanan asked to join us. I couldn't think of a reason to say no that didn't sound churlish."

"That's that creepy guy, isn't it? Why bother about sounding churlish?"

Tim shrugged and watched as Felix fumbled in his pocket for his wallet. He stopped at the bar set aside for sugar, stirrers and napkins and fumbled around in his pockets again while he was there.

Gillian giggled. "I hope he never needs a job as a waiter.

I've never seen anybody take so long to get from the counter to a table with three coffees."

"Don't forget the three cookies."

"That makes all the difference."

"Sorry for the wait," Felix said. "I couldn't remember which pocket I'd put my wallet in."

"No worries. We're in no rush. Gillian always likes to be early whether she's going by plane, train or automobile."

"Ha ha. Very good. The cappuccino is yours, I think, Gillian. Americano for Tim, and a refreshing Earl Grey Tea for me. I got us napkins for the cookies. I didn't think we needed plates."

"Oh, by the way, Bear was looking for you. Did he manage to speak to you before you left Lucky's?"

"Always good to speak with the big man," Felix said. "So, tell me about this trip to Russia, Gillian. Will you be safe there? Can you fly direct, or do you have to change in London?"

Tim smiled as Gillian started talking about her favourite topic, her trip to Moscow. He listened while she told Felix about the city, the university, the warm, funny people.

Tim ate his cookie and then Gillian's while Felix expressed interest in the language and culture of this country he had not seemed at all interested in any time Tim had seen him previously. He didn't like Felix monopolising this precious time with Gillian and was irritated with Gillian for letting it happen. They chatted for easily forty minutes without Tim getting a word in.

Gillian said she would go to the ladies' room before waiting in line at security, but as she stood up, she became pale. She sat back down again.

"Tim, I don't feel well. I feel so lightheaded. I feel all

wobbly. I can't get my legs to move properly. I can't see properly. Help me Tim."

Tim looked at her. Her skin had a grey sheen, and her skin was clammy to his touch.

"Felix, will you look after her while I find a medic?"

"Of course. I'll loosen her belt and top button. Poor girl looks ill. Go, Tim. Hurry."

Tim got up. He looked around but they had chosen a secluded table on purpose so they couldn't be seen, not that it made any difference after Felix joined them. Thank God that clown was there to look after her while he got medical attention.

He went up to the counter and ignored the coughing and complaining of the customers standing in line. He asked the server where he would find a doctor. The man looked at him blankly and told him he didn't know because he'd only started last Monday.

Tim saw a police officer parading up and down. He introduced himself and the man replied, "I knew your Dad. Right plonker, him, isn't he?"

"He can be, but right now I need medical assistance for my girlfriend. Is there a doctor in the airport?"

Just then he heard a bloodcurdling scream. "Gillian. That's Gillian," Tim ran towards her, and the officer followed him talking into his radio as they went.

They arrived just in time to find Felix standing over Gillian. Tim could see that he held her head firmly, but her body was limp. He held a Swiss army knife in one hand and what looked like escargot tongs in the other. She was unconscious and vulnerable.

"Felix!" Tim shouted.

There was no reply. No response. No sound. The man didn't even look round. It was as if he were in a demonic trance. The expression on his face was terrifying.

Tim leaped over the tables between him and Felix and rugby-tackled the man to the ground.

"I always knew you were weird, but I never knew you were a fucking monster."

The police officer walked around to Gillian. He felt her pulse. And lifted her eyelids.

"She's alive, but out cold. Like she's taken drugs or something," he said. "I've called for back-up and an ambulance, but in light of those moves maybe all you need are these." He handed Tim his handcuffs.

Tim pulled Felix to a standing position and growled the statement of his rights into his left ear.

"Careful, Tim remember, I've got a bad ankle."

"If I had my way, you'd have more than a bloody bad ankle. Why Felix? Why Gillian? Why anybody? It's the attack of a madman. The wickedness. Are you that man?"

Gillian slumped to the side and would have fallen to the floor if Tim hadn't loosened his hold on Felix and caught her. While he steadied her, he saw Felix running across the airport, showing little sign of that bad ankle he'd complained about, and the police officer was running after him. Tim decided to lie Gillian on the floor in the recovery position and then sprinted after Felix.

Tim caught up with Felix near the airport supermarket. "Did you really think that was going to work?"

"I had to try."

• • •

The officer was still breathless when he came up to Tim. “Paramedics are here. I’ve just taken them to your friend. They’ll take her to hospital to get checked over.”

“I don’t know which hospital is receiving A & E patients today.”

“Royal Infirmary.”

“Good. I’ll phone my sister she’s a registrar there. Will you go with Gillian in the ambulance? I must take this monster in for questioning. “Felix, you are under arrest, on suspicion of murder, assault to severe injury and anything else I can think of between now and when I get you to Fettes station. But before we go, call me ‘darling’.”

CHAPTER
FORTY-SEVEN

Eileen listened carefully to the first recording.

"No. That's not Frederick. That man has a foreign accent and Frederick's is local. He's well-spoken, much posher than me, but local."

Rachael never thought Mansoor would be the one, but that recording was there just to make sure.

"Okay, what about this next one?"

Eileen had a look of such concentration on her face, Rachael felt for her. The young woman was desperate to help.

"No, that voice is older and rougher than Frederick's. Frederick has a smooth voice almost musical."

"That's fine. Listen to this one."

Felix's voice filled the room. Rachael watched Eileen carefully. She watched the tears dribble from her tear ducts down her cheeks.

She nodded. "That's him. That's Frederick. Oh God, that's Frederick. Rachael, put it off I can't listen to it." She sobbed silently. "When you find out why he did this to me, will you tell me what he says?"

"I will, but I can tell you now, what I've told you before, he is a monster, and you did nothing wrong. But I must ask you to listen to one more voice, Eileen. It's for the sake of completeness and so that you have heard all of our suspects. Can you do that for me?"

"I will, but it won't be Frederick.

"No, that's not him. The voice isn't posh enough. The third one is Frederick. That may not be his real name, but that's Frederick."

Hunter walked into the incident room.

"Tim's gone to the hospital to be with Gillian, boss," Bear said.

"No problem. Find out the name of the officer who helped in the arrest. I want him to get the credit he's due. I'll also need a statement from him."

"PC Paul Wallace is his name is boss. He's coming in to give a statement tomorrow," Colin said.

"Please may I interview Felix, boss?" Bear asked.

"Would a negative answer hurt your feelings, DC Zewedu?"

"No but it might affect my dinner plans. I was going to tear that bastard limb from limb and marinade his testicles before barbecuing him piece by piece in flour and a blend of eleven herbs and spices."

"Which is exactly why you will stay here, and Oskar will come with me to interview Sir Felix Buchanan."

"Oskar's not even in the room." Mel complained.

"Because he's a DI and has his own room," Hunter said. "You all work on putting the case together for the Procurator

Fiscal. I don't want this one failing for want of anything we did or didn't do. Oskar and I will be in interview room one."

When Hunter and Oskar walked into the room, Della Maclehose was already sitting beside Felix.

"Now don't go throwing anybody under the bus. Remember, I act for both of you." Hunter heard her say.

"Sorry, Ms Maclehose, do you need a little more time with your client?"

"No. It's fine."

Hunter looked at the woman's long, elegant legs and expensive suit. Her hair was well coiffed and her nails highly manicured. Hunter thought he'd probably seen less make-up on a pantomime dame.

"Good. Would you or your client like something to drink? We could be some time."

"Water," Felix said.

"Water for both of us would be fine."

When the PC came back with the drinks, Hunter explained the recording system and introduced everybody in the room for the benefit of the tape. He also made clear that Felix was being interviewed under caution and with the benefit of legal representation.

"Now, Sir Felix, let's start with today. What is your version of events?"

"Remember you don't need to say anything," Della said.

"But we may consider your position if you refuse to answer all or any of our questions." Oskar added.

"I might as well tell them. It's not as if Tim saw nothing." Felix looked at Della who shrugged her shoulders and took up her pen.

"On your own head be it, but it is contrary to my advice."

"This morning when Lucky and I were playing video games McKellar came through and asked when it would be convenient for detectives to come and speak to me again and make a recording of my voice." Felix sighed. "I just had this horrible feeling that someone was going to share the sound with Eileen. I always thought it would have been better if she'd died too."

"I doubt she thinks so," Hunter said.

"I couldn't let it happen. I told McKellar to tell them they'd missed me, grabbed my passport and a change of clothes and drove out to the airport. I found a gig in Dublin looking for a celebrity DJ to take a turn and bought a ticket. I thought that would get me out of the country and nobody would find me at the airport. And who do I see but bloody Timothy Myerscough. Just my sodding luck."

"You could have avoided him, but you chose to approach him. Why?" Hunter asked.

"I remembered his girlfriend's eyes. They are the most beautiful shade of bright green. I have never seen eyes that colour and I knew Arjun would treasure them. I must work off my debt to him, but I don't know how. The interest keeps going up. I thought those eyes might do it."

"Really? You attack, murder and blind women to pay off a drug debt?"

"I never killed anyone."

"And my client didn't say what the debt was for," Della said.

"Was your debt to Mansoor as a result of his supply to you of class A drugs."

"I'm addicted to cocaine. Of course, it was. Mansoor is in

prison just now, so he doesn't supply anyone with anything directly."

Hunter noticed that Della relaxed a bit when Felix made this comment.

"I thought you were paying your drug debt by taking drugs into gigs for Mansoor's associates to distribute and you took the money to Mr Morrison for clearing," Hunter said.

"I couldn't say who the pushers were working for," Felix said.

"Good try, but why else would they collect their supply from the stuff you took into the gigs?" Hunter asked.

"Who did you get the stuff from in the first place? We know you took it in because you're a celebrity and wouldn't get searched." Oskar frowned. "But you had to have a supplier."

"I'd get a message telling me where to pick up the coke. Always a different number. Never with a name. It's good stuff, from Peru."

"I'm delighted to hear you only supplied good gear," Hunter said sarcastically. "But let's get back to the airport. Why did you approach Tim?"

"I thought if I took the coffees over, I might get a chance to look at Gillian's eyes again. If they were as beautiful as I remembered, I would have to have them for the collection. All I had to do was get rid of Tim for a few minutes."

"When Dr Ailsa Myerscough saw Gillian being brought into the hospital, she thought she might be drugged with the same stuff that incapacitated Eileen Maguire." Hunter looked closely at Felix who in turn was looking fixedly at the table. "We are running tests on Gillian's blood right now. Do you think she will be right?"

"It's possible. I'm not sure."

"I think it is more than possible and you are perfectly sure, Sir Felix. Are all the younger members of your family's generation rotten to the core, or just you?" Oskar asked.

"My client deserves courtesy, and his family does not deserve this slur. Retract the statement, Inspector."

"As soon as your client proves me wrong.

"Let me get this right," Hunter said. "You became addicted to coke."

"Yes, Lucky introduced me to it, but when he went into rehab, I couldn't get the money to pay for it and I ran up a debt to Arjun Mansoor. He's good at supplying people who have cash flow problems and then he has you in his power. He's done something for you, so you have to do something for him."

"An old trick, but a flawless logic," Hunter said.

Della stood up. "I regret that I cannot continue to represent Sir Felix. He is naming other clients of mine who are not here to defend themselves."

"I suspect he's only mentioned one, but the police constable will show you out, Ms. Maclehose. We'll suspend the interview. Would you like us to get another lawyer for you, Felix?" Hunter asked.

"I suppose it would be best. Can I go outside for a ciggie?"

"Come on. I'll go with you," Oskar said. He felt one pocket for his cigarettes and the other for his lighter as they made their way to the carpark.

When the interview recommenced, Andrew Barley had taken over the lawyer's seat.

"Good day, gentlemen. I have been briefed by my client. My advice is that he be as frank as possible with you and explain the whole sorry tale to you from beginning to end. He has admitted some terrible actions to me which have had devastating effects on his own life and those of other people, but there are mitigating circumstances. Sir Felix, over to you," Barley said.

"You know I was indebted to Arjun Mansoor. I told you that. He'd get his men to come and hound me, threaten me and beat me up. That's how I got the bad ankle, it wasn't running for the plane. I was running away from his goons after I got off the plane."

"He's in jail," Oskar said.

"I'm not brave and he has a long reach. He terrorises half the people in the jail. If a guy they call Thomson wasn't in there, Mansoor would be terrorising them all. That's what I've heard."

"Go on," said Hunter.

"Mansoor is fascinated by eyes. The mirrors of the soul, the smile of the heart. He especially likes unusual shades of eyes, the translucent appearance the eyes of some people with albinism, deep green eyes, bright blue eyes, and Eileen Maguire had genuinely violet eyes, just like Elizabeth Taylor did."

"Let's get back on track, never mind about film stars," Oskar said.

"No, it's important, it's all part of it."

"Carry on," said Hunter.

"Mansoor suggested first that I get pictures of people with unusual eye colours. He suggested going on a dating site might be a good place to start."

"How did he contact you?"

"By phone. It's true the number's never the same. Sometimes one of his henchmen would catch up with me and thump me. Then he'd whisper a suggestion into my ear as to how I could avoid getting beaten up, again."

"When was the first time he suggested that the people might have their eyes removed?"

"He told me his optician, Steven Morrison, wasn't really qualified, and Mansoor hadn't let the cat out of the bag, so the guy owed him. I was to take him a dead animal and he would remove the eyes and preserve them. It didn't sound too bad. Gruesome, but not illegal. When I found a dead cat at the side of the road, I took it to Morrison. I knew where he lived because of the envelopes of cash being delivered there. I didn't stay to watch, just dropped it off."

"Did you put a dead cat on his doorstep recently?"

"Just for fun." Felix laughed. "He's not a nice man, very dull. I thought it would be funny."

"He and his wife didn't find it fun, or funny," Oskar said. "And they blamed someone else. Who, in turn, was subjected to a police interview."

"I don't care."

"I didn't think you would."

"I need a drink and a cigarette."

"I don't care," said Oskar.

Hunter suspended the interview and watched Andrew Barley as he went outside to the car park with Felix. Hunter and Oskar went into Hunter's room.

"Want a decent coffee while we have a chance, Oskar?"

"Thanks. I have a feeling that the next bit of the story might require more than coffee to swallow it. Is Mansoor really as bad as Felix is making out?"

"Every time I hear his name, it always has wicked connotations. But Felix is right about Ian Thomson keeping Mansoor in check inside."

"Doesn't that make more problems for him?"

"Only if he gets caught."

Bear stormed into Hunter's room. "Is that slug still here? I've just heard from Tim. Do you know what that fucking monster tried to do to Gillian? She's out cold from whatever drug he gave her, and the right side of her face is all scratched because he tried to scoop her fucking eyes out."

Hunter stared at Bear. "DC Zewedu, it would be nice if you knocked before entering my office when I'm in a meeting."

"Ten minutes. Just give me ten frigging minutes, boss. I'll give fucking Sir Felix just what he deserves."

"Bear, take the rest of the day off. Go for a walk or run until your temper is back to normal and I'll see you tomorrow."

"I'll run to the door of the fucking estate and wait for that bastard until he gets there."

"Under no circumstances will you go within ten miles of the Buchanan estate. Calm down Bear. Oskar and I have got this. Now get out of here."

Hunter didn't move until Bear left his office. He then looked at Oskar and shook his head. "Bear and Tim have been friendly since they were eleven. They are great friends, and loyal protectors. Bear will rumble all night, but he'll see things more calmly in the morning. Now we better get back to that interview. Lead the way, Oskar."

Hunter recommenced the interview. "Sir Felix, so far you have told us that both you and Steven Morrison were indebted to Arjun Mansoor for different reasons and that initially you were only required to take a dead animal to Mr Morrison to allow him to harvest and preserve the eyes. The evidence found at his former home would support that claim.

"You also say that Mr Mansoor wanted you to join dating websites and supply him with pictures of women with unusual eye colours. When did that change to you attacking the women to drug them and harvest their eyes?"

"Not immediately. At first, I would just meet up with girls at my gigs and if they had eyes that I knew Arjun would like, I'd get them drunk or high and take photos to send him."

"That's what happened in Ibiza. She wasn't drunk enough and complained."

"Something must have changed. Two women are dead, one is blind and another assaulted and scarred," Oskar said.

"The first two weren't me. But I was there. I met them through a dating site, and Mansoor's men supplied me with Rohypnol. They told me to get them high with the drug and to take the first one for a walk in the woods and the second for a walk along the beach.

On both occasions we were jumped. I don't know who by, but it must have been Mansoor's men because I was held and made to watch while they butchered the women's heads and took their eyes. When they were finished, I was released and instructed to take the eyes to Steven.

"The eyes were in containers with liquid. I don't know what. The women didn't move. I thought they were dead. I ran. I just fucking ran.

"I kept vomiting when the visions came back to me. But I never killed anyone. Although it might have been better if my one died too. It was so inconvenient; this was all bound to come out."

"Are you admitting the attack on Eileen Maguire which has resulted in her being blinded?"

"Yep. I suppose I must. I had to get out from the scene really fast, because some bloody nosy police officer found her in the lift and so I got away through the public bar and got a bus back to the Morrisons' place."

"Why did you go to the Morrison's house?"

"I was told to put her eyes in a container this goon gave me and get them to Morrisons' for preservation as quickly as possible. I'm dreadfully sorry for what I did to Eileen. But I had no choice, I had to pay Mansoor back for my drugs."

"I doubt she'll be too forgiving about that," Hunter said.

CHAPTER FORTY-EIGHT

JAMIE WAS PLEASED WITH HIS NEW HOME. IT WAS MUCH MORE peaceful than next door where the twins ran around and shrieked with laughter or anger, depending on their mood. Some of their furniture had come from Eileen's flat in Tollcross and the new furniture was delivered from Ikea, and he watched Linda put it all together while he held the instruction and the screws.

"I've never met a man who doesn't even own a screwdriver or a hammer, much less a toolbox," she said.

"I don't need one. I've got you and you've got a toolbox. And you're doing a great job putting all this together."

"Thanks. I'm not going to put the stuff together for Eileen's room, or your Pop's. It'll be some months before Eileen's finished her rehab and can move in and who knows when your pop'll be out and able to join us. I don't like to think what he'd do to Arjun Mansoor if he gets hold of him in the big house."

"That thought's all that keeps me going, Linda. As long as Pop doesn't get caught in the act. I think we should get Eileen's room put together, though. I'd like it done before she comes for her recce visit tomorrow."

"I like your use of the word 'we', but you're probably right. I'll take a loo break and you unpack Eileen's bed, wardrobe and chair then we'll get it done. I think it'll be good for her having her own things. Did we remember the cat basket and the dog's bed?"

"Of course. Eileen can decide if she wants them in her room or downstairs. I don't mind, I quite like Princess Leia and Rory."

"That's good. But you'll have to get tea for us tonight. I'll be too tired."

"No problem. Fish and chips or pizza?" Jamie grinned at Linda and went down to the kitchen to get them a couple of diet cokes from the fridge. He was pleased with the results of their choices and believed Eileen would settle in well with them.

Eileen was nervous. This was the first time she'd have visited her new home. She had lived alone with her cat for so long, that she would have to get used to living with other people.

The little flat she'd had in Tollcross had sold quickly and given her a nest egg and Linda and Jamie seemed keen to have her stay with them. She hoped her company wouldn't get old too fast for them.

Her furniture had been moved into their new home and what she didn't have, they'd bought. It would be nice to have some familiar things around her, even if she couldn't see them.

There was a knock on the door. "Hello, Eileen, it's Rachael. May I come in?"

"Yes, of course."

"I brought you a little house-warming gift. It's a gardenia. I thought you might enjoy the perfume. But I brought some chocolates too."

Eileen smiled. "The plant smells lovely, but you can never go wrong with chocolate."

"It won't be too long until you and Rory move into your new home in West Mains Road."

"No, it won't, and Rory has met Princess Leia several times now and they seem to get on fine. If Jamie stops tripping over the cat, and Linda stops fussing and lets me make my own tea, everything will be great.

"I can walk to the local shops and get a bus from just round the corner to work when I get started on my new job. My life will be different to the one I had, but at least I still have one. The first two women that were attacked died, didn't they?"

"Yes, they did. Their main attackers have been caught too and they're in jail awaiting trial. The man who attacked you was also present at those murders."

"It's shocking, he's nobility or something, Sir Felix Buchanan, they told me. How could he do that? Aren't those kinds of people meant to set an example? He even tried to lay the blame on someone else, a guy who's already in jail. He's just scum. Well, he may have changed my life, but he's not going to ruin it."

"He won't be back on the streets any time soon. He did say he was sorry for you."

"Sorry for himself that I lived and could identify his voice more like. Bastard."

"Agreed. Shall we go for a walk around the grounds for some fresh air?" Rachael asked.

"I'm just waiting for Noah to bring Rory over then I'm going for a walk around the neighbourhood to see if I can manage with Rory on my own. Noah is going to walk behind me, just in case I need him."

"Did I hear someone mention my name?" Noah walked into the room with Rory. The dog's tail was wagging, and he went straight up to Eileen. "Hello Rachael. If all goes well today, Rory will be moving in to stay with Eileen permanently. They have both completed their training and work really well together."

"Congratulations. Well done Eileen. I'll leave you now, but you have my number, if you ever want a chat, or to go for a coffee or anything, just give me a call." Rachael shook Noah's hand and kissed Eileen lightly on the cheek. "Nothing will stop you now."

Rachael hurried away. If she were lucky, she'd manage to speak to Hunter before this morning's briefing. It was important to get him to put her request in before the deadline.

CHAPTER FORTY-NINE

"It doesn't seem like two months since we were last here," Gillian said. "I always used to like airports and traveling, but I'm finding today so stressful, Tim."

"I know. Don't worry, I've bought myself a ticket to London too."

"You're not coming with me, are you?"

"No." Tim smiled. "I'm not coming with you, but it allows me to go through security with you and see you safely to the gate for your flight. I'm not taking any chances."

"Thank you. One of my new colleagues is meeting me in Boryspil International Airport, so I only have to navigate Heathrow, and I know that airport well enough."

"Don't talk to any strange, bearded men. That's all I ask. I will miss you, you know."

"I'll miss you too, but you will come to visit, won't you? You could come for your winter skiing trip. There is good alpine skiing and snowboarding at Rosa Khutor."

"That sounds like a great idea. I'm glad you want me to come. I've never been skiing in Russia. In fact, I've never been to the country at all. Let me know when you have time off and we'll get it arranged. Look, your plane is leaving from gate 12. Let's go."

Tim took Gillian's hand and they walked along the corridor to the gate. He stood and watched until she entered the airbridge and he could no longer see her. Then he turned and walked back to the airport terminus and drove to the station for the morning briefing.

CHAPTER
FIFTY

"Good of you to take the time to join us, DC Myerscough," Hunter said.

"I was dropping Gillian at the airport, boss. I'm not late, am I?"

"Nearly." Hunter smiled. "Now, Rachael, you first. How is Eileen?"

"She's a lovely woman, boss. She's having her final training day with her guide dog today and then she'll be moving out of rehab and into the house Jamie and Linda have bought for the three of them. I think she's quite looking forward to the move, getting back to work and starting what will be her new normal."

"That's all good news. Did you tell her we've caught the beasts that murdered the other women?"

"Yes boss. I also told her Felix won't be out on the streets any time soon. She was pleased about that and determined not to let what happened to her ruin her life, just change it."

"She's certainly brave. How's Gillian, Tim?"

"Physically she's fine, boss but she was nervous about

going back to Edinburgh Airport. When I thought about it, we should have done a dummy run before today, but we didn't. Anyway, she's on the plane to Heathrow and someone is meeting her in Moscow, so she'll be fine."

"Good. What do we know about Morrison, Nadia?"

"I've informed The General Optical Council that he's been acting as an optician without being qualified to practice and they've informed all their members of the fraud. He won't be doing that again."

"I wonder what Hector thought about his uncle naming him as the attacker?"

"I'd like to have been a fly on the wall when that came out," Nadia said.

"What has Morrison been charged with?" Hunter asked.

"Aiding and abetting assault to severe injury, because although he didn't take part in any of the assaults, he knew about them and did nothing to stop them. We've also got him for helping to launder the drug money. That's what we found in Hector and John's flat and office. His professional body will deal with the rest."

"That sounds like Morrison will get the book thrown at him. Good. And what about Mansoor, Colin?"

"Sentencing next week, but he'll get time added. There's no doubt about that and the Procurator Fiscal also intends to prosecute John Hamilton for the drugs and cash we found. But I don't know about Hector."

"I don't know either, but I doubt he'll get off entirely." Hunter nodded. "It depends on how much he is found to have known about what was going on."

"What about Felix?" Bear asked. "I never liked that man."

Hunter looked around his team. "He's named in the two

murder cases, being prosecuted for the attacks on Eileen and Gillian. He's in for a long haul."

"Not as long a haul as Eileen," Rachael said.

"She'll be sorry to hear you're leaving us to join MIT. But our new Detective Sergeant Myerscough will have to give evidence in the assault case against Gillian."

A cheer went up around the room.

Bear jumped to his feet and shook Tim warmly by the hand. "When did you sit the exam? When did you hear? That's great news."

"The drinks are on Tim." Mel grinned.

"I'm not buying all the drinks," Tim said. "Let me introduce our new DCI Hunter Wilson who is engaged to be married to the amazing Dr Meera Sharma. Congratulations, boss."

COMING SOON

Hunter's Festival follows soon

ACKNOWLEDGMENTS

Writing is often portrayed as a solitary occupation, but while this story is the product of one mind, the process of creating a book is far from solitary.

First may I thank my long-suffering beta-readers who took the time to read an early draft, give critique and endorsements, Particular mention goes to Hennie McClure for her helpful suggestions and improvements. I am also most grateful to Stewart Penny who continues to advise on fitness and exercise for my characters.

My editors Laurence Paterson and Nikki East are amongst the most patient people I have ever met. Their helpful observations and eye for detail improved this novel immeasurably. The team at SpellBound are supportive and show their belief in me even when I am at my lowest ebb.. Thanks must also go to Sumaira Wilson who polished the blurb for Hunter's Rules. Without SpellBound this book would not exist. Of course, all errors are mine.

My beloved husband, Dave, deserves a special mention for his unconditional support and encouragement. I am also lucky to enjoy enthusiasm for my work from our dear girls, Lizzie and Vicky, Rebecca and Lily.

Above all, to each and every one of my readers, thank you. You make my job worthwhile.

ABOUT THE AUTHOR

Val Penny has an Llb degree from the University of Edinburgh and her MSc from Napier University. She has had many jobs including hairdresser, waitress, banker, azalea farmer and lecturer but has not yet achieved either of her childhood dreams of being a ballerina or owning a candy store.

Until those dreams come true, she has turned her hand to writing poetry, short stories, nonfiction books, and novels. Her novels are published by SpellBound Books Ltd.

Val is an American author living in SW Scotland. She has two adult daughters of whom she is justly proud and lives with her husband and their cat.

ALSO BY VAL PENNY

HUNTER'S CHASE

HUNTER'S REVENGE

HUNTER'S FORCE

HUNTER'S BLOOD

HUNTER'S SECRET

HUNTER'S CHRISTMAS

SERIES DOWNLOAD LINK HERE !

Printed in Great Britain
by Amazon

44234325R00169